Secrets of Gra:

A ghost mystery set in Lincolnshire,
England, United Kingdom.

The second of the
James Hansone Ghost Mysteries

By Paul Money

Secrets of Grasceby Manor

Copyright Notice

Astrospace Publications
18 College Park, Horncastle, Lincolnshire LN9 6RE
www.astrospace.co.uk

Copyright © Paul Money February 2016 / POD October 2020
All rights reserved.

The right of Paul Money to be identified as the author of this work has been asserted by him in accordance with the Copyright, Designs and Patents Act 1988.

All the characters in the story are fictional and any resemblance to real persons either living or dead is purely coincidental.
No part of this book may be reproduced in any form other than that which it was purchased and without the written permission of the author.
This e-book is licensed for your personal enjoyment only.
This ebook may not be re-sold or given away to other people in either this or any other format.

Language: UK English

Cover:
Principal designer: Cupit/Rebecca Turner
Based on original ideas by Paul Money

Cover photos:
fotolia.com
© david hughes © IRStone © lynea istockphoto.com © duncan1890

Acknowledgements

The author would like to acknowledge the support and help of his wife, Lorraine, in listening to the idea of the third sequel, how it developed and giving both invaluable advice, encouragement and editing ideas as the story progressed.

He would also like to thank the following for their advice, informed wisdom, patience, and encouragement as this book progressed from a few pages to a full-blown novel:

Gill Hart
Mark Lenton
Jane Annetts
Pat and Keith Money (Mum & Dad)
Margaret Slater (Mum 2 aka Mum in Law)
Sally Wood
Rebecca Turner

And finally acknowledge the wonderful help and support of Cupit Print of Horncastle for their work on the original print edition and cover for both the original printed edition and the e-pub POD editions.

Preface

Renovations at the Manor
A mysterious upper class gentleman in Grasceby Churchyard
A ghostly boy
A servant called Annie
A 150 year old conspiracy

James Hansone thought he was done with ghosts once he'd discovered the truth about his family.

He was mistaken.

Grasceby Manor stands in several acres of old landscaped gardens and had been the jewel of the village.

But now it desperately needed renovation, prompting Lord Grasceby to hire a local firm to renovate the property in readiness of the opening of parts of it to the public. But as work commences, strange sightings of a boy and a servant girl begin to occur to the workman and James finds himself increasingly drawn into trying to discover:
The identity of the boy.

The connection to the ghostly servant.

Whether he can find out who or what caused their deaths.

And why a cat seems determined to trip him up!

Prologue

1843 - 1864

Annie stood and looked around, then smiled as her cat allowed her to pick him up. She climbed the steps and carried it back up to her small but cosy room on the top floor of Grasceby Manor. She placed a small saucer of milk on the wooden floor and he lapped the contents up with glee as Annie sat on the edge of her bed, knowing that life was as good as it could possibly be. She thought back on how lucky she was; Lord and Lady Grasceby were gracious, kind and considerate employers and she reflected on the stories she had heard about how they were the exception rather than the rule when it came to looking after their employees.

Due to their kindness and generosity, their head housekeeper, Audrey, had proved fiercely loyal. When she died whilst giving birth, the Lord and Lady were so distressed that they instructed Mrs Bottomly, 'Cook', to ensure the newly arrived baby Annie was cared for and looked after as one of their own.

Although raised as a servant, Annie was considered their special ward and so was lucky enough to be well fed, even to be educated, being taught to read and write. As she entered into her late teens, Lady Grasceby's brother, Lord Silverwright, took a shine to her when he visited on his rare trips to see his sister and brother-in-law.

As she sat on her small but reasonably comfortable bed, she chuckled and blushed slightly as she remembered his somewhat nervous attempts at conversation.

However, nothing untoward occurred due to his position and prominence, scandals were not to be encouraged regardless of the circumstances or temptation.

Meanwhile, not for the want of trying, their lord and ladyship remained childless. Then when they had all but given up hope, in their late thirties their prayers were answered and a boy was born to them. Christened George, his birth almost cost Lady Charlotte her life as history tried to repeat itself, but her ladyship clung on and came out of the birth a stronger woman. Their physician, Doctor Frederickson, was a close friend who helped them through the birth and this fraught time as her ladyship regained her strength and the child survived.

Annie again smiled to herself and remembered how proud she had been when George was placed in her care when her ladyship had to be away from the manor. She loved little George like a brother. From that moment on she was determined that nothing should ever happen to him. The bond between them grew yet didn't affect George's love of his parents whom he was beginning to understand were important people. He cherished the times he had with both his mother and with Annie.

Annie tapped her lap on seeing her cat had finished his milk. He obligingly leapt up, snuggled in, and began to purr as Annie wondered about the new people the good doctor had recently introduced to the Grasceby's, the Cordings of Wragby. By the sound of it they had fallen on hard times, not, you understand, that Annie ever listened in on private conversations. Little did she, nor Lord and Lady Grasceby, know that the 'good' doctor always felt the Grascebys owed him for saving Charlotte and George's lives and it wasn't long before he began to consider his options for advancement.

And so, an unlikely trio began to plot and plan.

Slowly. Painfully slowly it seemed to the ever impatient Mrs Cording, the strands began to come together as step by step the groundwork was laid.

Ready for the takeover of Grasceby Manor ...

1: A sad day

"We are gathered here on this day to say farewell to Michael Stephen Freshman who tragically passed away whilst on holiday. It is perhaps a small consolation to us all who knew him that he was taken as he enjoyed his favourite pastime, fishing in his beloved Scotland. Michael left us on January twelfth this year aged sixty eight, it was a shock to us all considering he always appeared to have a cast iron constitution and rarely fell ill."

The Reverend Sarah Cossant paused in her delivery, looking over the assembled mass, then briefly consulted the notes carefully laid out on the pulpit before continuing. "Detective superintendent Freshman, or 'Mike' to his friends, will be remembered fondly as our local retired detective, always willing to go that extra mile, be it in his work or after he retired, especially in his local community efforts. He was a popular man who never married, but who gathered friends like lost sheep and helped them in whatever way he could. He…"

James felt Sally's hand tighten in his and she trembled slightly. He knew this day would be difficult for her, as she had studied and trained under her former mentor. It was still hard to believe he was now gone from their lives. Mike had been at first reluctant, then enthusiastic about bringing Sally and James together when the latter's marriage to Helen had fallen apart the previous year due to unusual circumstances.

He had a canny knack of knowing when two people suited each other and he'd been right about them. He'd also frequently reminded them of that fact as well, much to their amusement and slight embarrassment.

Mike had also been one of the few people to believe James when he found he could see the ghost of a young girl called Jenny. She had been missing for over fifty years from Wolds View cottage on the outskirts of the sleepy village of Grasceby in central Lincolnshire, but with James' help, Mike and Sally solved Jenny's missing persons case.

The effect on James' marriage was profound though, as his wife Helen began an affair with his work colleague Craig and, citing the ghost as unreasonable behaviour on James' part, the couple had separated after what had seemed like a happy twenty years of marriage. Helen moved away to Nottingham to be with her lover whilst James remained in their home in Horncastle. Both sides were waiting for the divorce to be finalised, the paperwork confirming the divorce was not expected to arrive for some time, such being the slow nature of legal matters.

As the weeks had passed, James and Sally had become close and were shocked to discover that Jenny had actually been James' sister. In a complicated twist, James' mother, Barbara, was also Jenny's mother. When Jenny went missing all those years ago, Jack, her father, died almost a year later of what some said was a broken heart.

Soon afterwards, an expectant Barbara moved away from Lincolnshire and had changed her name. She did this before James was born so they both could have a fresh start. Therefore James had grown up never knowing his father and not knowing that he should have had a sister.

All that seemed a long time ago since James had discovered the truth when his mother passed away. Even though it was eight months ago it was still difficult for James to come to terms with the fact that his mother, whom he had known all his life as Mary Hansone, had hidden a secret past. And now Mike was also dead. A fishing trip to Scotland had gone tragically wrong when his boat capsized in Loch Bunachton one cold and foggy morning. Everyone thought he was a good swimmer but it was only at the coroner's inquest, it was concluded that he'd suffered a heart attack, probably due to shock, when he fell into the icy cold water.

Sally loosened her grip and nodded appreciatively at James as the Reverend continued with the service.

'Abide with me' and 'The Lord is my Shepherd' came and went along with solemn words and memories from many of Mikes former colleagues, although Sally couldn't bear to bring herself to stand in front of everybody and speak. It wasn't long before they were filing out, handing over donations and a few making their way to the grave side. Mike's coffin was carried along by several former colleagues from the police force and as Mike had no family left, James and Sally followed on behind.

Gently, Mike's coffin was lowered into the freshly dug grave, they each took it in turns to throw a handful of soil onto it, bow their heads and step back as the Reverend Cossant gave the last of her prayers.

James was always one to let his thoughts roam during sad occasions such as this, he reflected that Mike had insisted in his will on a traditional funeral and burial. He had told James he had been against being cremated when, in a poignant moment a few weeks earlier, they had been sitting in his front lounge. Somehow the discussion had turned to life, death and of course ghostly apparitions. Although both were confirmed sceptics of the paranormal, Mike and Sally had to agree that James' own personal experiences were at odds with their 'scientific' views. Somehow in their deliberations they had got around to how each would want to be both remembered and buried.

James shuddered at the memory. Sally tightened her grip and looked at him with concern. He knew that ever since they'd found out that Mike was dead, she'd wondered if James would 'see' him as a ghost, as he'd 'seen' his sister. James smiled gently at her and they stayed until everyone else had left. They stood in silent contemplation, lost in their own thoughts. It was Sally who broke the silence first.

"They said at the inquest he probably knew little about it when he fell in." She said to no one in particular. She looked at James and appeared to be biting her lower lip. "You'll tell me if you see him, won't you?"

He nodded. "Of course love. I promise. I somehow don't think I will see him though. Jenny was family, even though at the time I didn't know it. I suspect that's why I saw her."

He looked around and realised the church groundsman was hanging around watching them. "Come on love, we'd better let Harry do his job. Let's come back in a day or two and pay our respects if you want." She smiled grimly and nodded. James turned to her and hesitated slightly. "After we've been to the reception at the inn, would you mind if we drive over to Grasceby? I just feel that I'd like to visit Jenny's grave."

"Of course, I gather Marcus has been busy over at the Star and Crescent Moon, so we ought to show our faces there for a little while. It was after all Mike's favourite watering hole." She smiled, took his hand again and led him back to the car leaving Harry to begin the task of finishing Mike's grave.

#

They gave their excuses after what seemed like hundreds of people talking to them about their memories of Mike. Sally was glad to be leaving the inn at last. It was only a few minutes drive to Grasceby church, soon they were standing at what James now knew as his family's grave. He still felt odd after discovering that he should have been christened James Portisham rather than James Hansone but the latter was the adopted name his mother had chosen so James Hansone he was and would remain.

With some persuasion he'd managed to arrange for his mother's body to be brought back to where she originally belonged. Now, in death, the family were back together again; mother, father and daughter, the Portishams of Grasceby.

He tidied up the now dead flowers he'd placed in the vase a few weeks back, promised the three graves he'd come back with some fresh ones soon. Sally stood slightly back from him to give him some space and looked over towards the church tower with the large doors at their base. They were almost alone, a gentleman wearing a top hat and long dark overcoat was standing near the entrance and seemed to glance their way briefly before looking off into the distance. She stepped closer to James and put her arm around his waist. He turned to her and smiled then looked up past her quizzically. Sally followed his gaze and almost jumped out of her skin, the gentleman with the top hat was standing just a couple of feet from them now.

"Good day to you, I apologise if I startled you Ma'am, it was not intentional I can assure you."

The gentleman had taken off his top hat and gave them both a slight bow. He put his hat back on and looked James squarely in the eyes. "May I enquire sir, if you be James Portisham?" James stepped back a little at the mention of the surname, very few actually knew that should have been his original surname.

"Err well yes and no, – it's very complicated. And you are?" He managed to stammer as he regained his composure.

"You'll forgive me sir, but I have to be quick for now. Let us say that a mutual acquaintance of ours recommended you to me. I require use of your services sir as I am taken to believe you can, let us say, communicate or see the dead?"

Both James and Sally were taken aback by this. James stepped towards the man. "I'm sorry but you seem to have been misled and our so-called mutual friend should not have said anything of the sort to you. I'm not a ghost hunter or whatever at all and I'd rather not think about such things, thank you very much." James turned as if to leave but the gentleman quickly stepped in front of him.

"Please sir do forgive my abruptness, I only wish you to hear what I have to say and if the answer is no then I will bid you and thy dear lady farewell and I will not trouble you again." Top hat held in front of him against his chest, the gentleman's pleading tone caused James to waiver, but Sally had other ideas.

"Sir, my partner has made his feelings quite clear. I am a police officer and I am asking you to leave us alone." James loved it when Sally got all official like this but he held her arm gently and turned to the gentleman.

"I'll give you a minute to tell me what it is you want and no more."

The gentleman bowed slightly.

"My nephew used to live at Grasceby Manor but vanished with no trace at all. I tried to discover what became of him to no avail. I believe he may have been, shall we say, disposed of, but alas I was prevented from discovering the truth by unfortunate and unforeseeable circumstances.

I hoped that you may stand a better chance than I of discovering what may have become of him and..." at that moment the Church clock began to chime to announce it was 3pm and the gentleman looked pained.

James shook his head. "I'm sorry but this is really a police matter and as I said I'm not a ghost hunter, I'm sure it is being dealt with in the right hands, eh Sally?" She nodded in agreement.

"Any investigation can take months and even years to come to fruition depending upon the circumstances. I'm sure the officer in charge has it in hand but I'm not aware of anything to do with a young boy going missing locally. I assume it has been reported?" she said. The gentleman looked resigned but again performed a slight bow to them both.

"I am so sorry to have troubled you. I was mistaken. Enjoy your day."

He turned and strolled purposefully along the path back towards the church entrance. James shook his head at the abruptness of this and with Sally, turned to head back along the path towards where the car was parked. "I didn't get his name in the end.", said James. He turned to call after the gentleman but he was already gone from sight. Sally looked a little puzzled.

"Wow – that was quick. Odd really as I'm usually the first to know if someone has gone missing and other than Jenny, I figure I know most of the current missing persons cases. Mind you he looked like an escapee from the local am dram group.

Odd chap but quite polite really – pity more people couldn't be like that even if he was a little weird."

James chuckled in agreement and they headed off to the car as the clock bell finished striking 3pm.

2: Grasceby Manor

Grasceby Manor was a three storey high, stately looking building with several outbuildings that were originally stables and workshops. It dominated Grasceby village and was surrounded by a brick wall almost seven feet tall. This was a throw back to a previous Lord being somewhat shy, of a nervous disposition and hating public attention, not that he could actually escape from it.

The manor was also situated in almost two acres of garden, a small fraction of which lay at the front and most of the rest at the rear with vegetable patches and flower beds.

It had been built not long after the first manor, the De Grasceby Manor, had been abandoned and fallen into ruin. It was rumoured that the first Lord De Grasceby fled back to France from where he and his family had originally hailed.

That lord, Charles De Grasceby, had been a wealthy French aristocrat who relocated from Paris with his family to the farming county of Lincolnshire in England in 1716.

This was contrary to normal practice because of the hatred between the two countries and quite an exception, although Charles had always been somewhat vociferous in his opinions. The prevailing theory maintained that De Grasceby had been publicly against the French attempt at crowning the Old Pretender, James Stuart, as King of England in 1715.

This move saw him become unpopular in his own country and explained why he was allowed to come over to Lincolnshire by the eventually crowned King George I.

The King awarded him with an estate and an allowance for his loyal support.

In the meantime, De Grasceby had salvaged a good proportion of his wealth by smuggling many valuables out of France across the channel via a friendly Lincolnshire based ally. With this wealth he commissioned the building of a grand manor situated between Horncastle, Wragby and Bardney for his remaining family, along with a few dwellings nearby for his servants.

The latter becoming the original site for Grasceby village. Local accounts soon after suggested the Manor was only partially completed however, as it soon became clear that Charles was a wanton gambler and lost most of the estate lands he'd been given by the King, along with a large part of his fortune. The family struggled whilst living in the unfinished manor and gradually their servants abandoned them to seek better employment elsewhere.

When George II succeeded his father to the throne in 1727, the new King had no love for De Grasceby, detesting the Frenchman. De Grasceby fled England but records of where he and his family went were lost in time with no one knowing what became of them. Popular myth had it that the Frenchman and his family drowned when their ship sank whilst crossing the North Sea but some rumours suggested they had been murdered by a local squire wanting the money he was owed.

Meanwhile, left unattended and unwanted, the manor fell into disrepair, never to be used again. The nearby village also deteriorated as people left, but a few loyal villagers moved to a new, better located site nearby and founded the modern village of Grasceby using stone scavenged from both the original village and the manor. The modern Grasceby Manor was constructed almost ten years after the foundation of the new village and, apart from a few internal renovations, largely remained unchanged on the outside. When De Grasceby fled, George II eventually awarded the estate lands, including the village of Grasceby, to his loyal followers, the Ferrymores of Kingston upon Hull who became Lord and Lady Grasceby in 1738.

But today times have changed and the current Lord Grasceby had been forced to accept that if he wished to continue to hold on to his estate and manor then he had to do something several of his colleagues across the country had already resorted to – opening parts of his home to the public. So began the renovation and preparation of the manor to receive visitors. Now, Jack Hammonds and his small but dedicated team were assessing and working on several of the rooms at Grasceby Manor to ready them for the grand opening later in the summer.

It was no mean task as decades of slow neglect had taken it's toll, in particular, on the rather unusual wooden panelled walls on the second floor hallway. The ground floor study and the basement fared a little better but still needed work to make them usable and presentable to the public.

Jack had estimated only a third of the manor would actually be open to the public, with several downstairs rooms, including the Study and the upper floors where his Lord and Ladyship lived along with their daughter, remaining private.

Phil was Jack's plasterer and stood in the doorway of the kitchen looking into the hallway, contemplating which room to tackle next. Meanwhile, his bucket steadily filled with water in the kitchen sink. Phil's motto was – 'don't do it too quick but do it right nonetheless!' He shivered as he felt a cold draft, for a split second he could have sworn something had actually passed through him. He shook his head and turned to go back into the kitchen to stop the tap flowing and halted in his tracks. The small boy looked at him, or it seemed to Phil, more like through him. He turned to look back at what the boy appeared to be looking at, realised he had not heard the boy come in; turning back, there was no one in the kitchen. Phil frowned and looked about. "Now little one, no playing games, I've got work to do an' the boss won't be happy if we don't keep to schedule and neither will your father."

Phil walked round the centre kitchen table expecting the boy to try to surprise him, perhaps playing hide and seek, but there was no one there. He looked at the back door seeing it was slightly ajar, he realised the lad must have sneaked out quietly. He shrugged his shoulders, fetched his bucket out of the sink as he realised it was overflowing and shaking his head in puzzlement, he headed back out into the hallway to go to the study.

A whisper of a voice made him stop and look around as he could have sworn someone had whispered 'Annie' behind him, but he was alone in the hallway. Phil frowned and was about to head into the study when the front door suddenly swung open, startling him. Lord Grasceby entered with a briefcase in one hand and his overcoat across his other arm. His Lordship smiled and nodded at Phil as he was about to pass.

"Excuse me sir, just met your son, seems quite a shy one that, didn't stay to chat. I actually thought you had a daughter or at least that's what the boss told me."

Lord Grasceby stopped and looked at Phil with a puzzled expression.

"Son? I don't have one, a daughter, yes indeed, Heather, but no, no son sadly; wasn't to be I'm afraid. Heather is all we've got bless her, nine now and I have to say a bit precocious as well, but then, aren't they all at that age?" He chuckled and started to walk away as Phil thought briefly about this.

"Err, a girl, nine you say? Nope – this was a lad about seven or eight years at most I'd say, light brownish hair and so high." He gestured with his right hand indicating the height and now it was Lord Grasceby's turn to be puzzled.

"No definitely not, can't even think of anybody I know with a child that age and description. You must have imagined it. Either that or you chaps are letting anyone come in and roam about the place, heaven forbid. I do hope that's not the case you know?"

"Er no, of course not, I must have been mistaken, it was a quick look when I think about it. Sorry to have bothered you, sir." With that Phil walked away quickly and into the study but felt disturbed by what had transpired. It certainly must have looked that way as his younger colleague, Simon, looked up as Phil came in.

"You look blooming white as a sheet, you OK Phil?"

"I don't know, damndest thing just happened. I reckon I've seen a ghost in the kitchen."

This made Simon stop suddenly and glanced at his colleague intensely. "Kidding, right?"

Phil looked at him and changed tack. "Yeah, gottacha didn't I!" Simon shrugged and stuck his tongue out at him as Phil play-swiped his hand over the younger person's head. Simon got back to work as Phil carried his bucket over to the table but Phil's mind was on something other than work.

#

A couple of days later Phil's boss, Jack, asked him to check out the basement and old cellar to see what he thought regarding tidying them up to make it useable again for long term storage. They were forgotten rooms that had fallen into disuse. Now Lord Grasceby wanted to use them to store items useful for the tourist season, so he'd added them to the slowly increasing list of jobs they had to undertake.

Mind you his Lordship had cheekily argued that it was part of the overall renovations anyway and so expected no extra charge.

Jack insisted however that materials would have to be paid for otherwise the work wouldn't get done and, grudgingly, his Lordship agreed. Which is why Phil was now down in the basement examining the walls and sizing up how much plaster it would take to cover them. A big job he reckoned and stepped back to appreciate the scale of it.

'Air sure is cold down here' he muttered to no one. He knew that these sorts of basement had been ideal places for the Victorians to store food for long term keep. No fridges in those days and he chuckled to himself as he turned to go up the stone steps running up one side of the stone wall.

A brief flicker of movement made him turn back but there was nothing and he turned to head back up …

… just as the boy walked down the steps and through him, turned almost through a right angle then carried on until he almost reached the wall on the far side of the basement where he faded from view. Phil spun round to watch and began cursing before rushing up the steps and out into the hallway where he clattered into Lady Amelia Grasceby who screamed with shock. They both picked themselves up off the floor as Phil tried to both help her and calm her down as well but with little success. Jack burst in from outside whilst his lordship rushed down the stairs from the second floor and together they confronted the hapless Phil.

"What the hell is going on here and what have you done to my wife?" his lordship demanded to know.

Phil could only splutter and try to get his words out.

"Speak up man, explain yourself before I have you sacked!"

"The, the boy, a boy, there was a boy down there. He, he WALKED THROUGH ME!" Phil was shaking whilst Lord Grasceby scowled and turned to make sure his wife was all right. Jack just glared at Phil.

"What do you mean, walked through you? You mean it was a ghost?" he demanded.

"Yes, that's it, just like the other day in the kitchen, it went cold both times. He's quite young..."

Lord Grasceby sniffed Phil's breath. He was satisfied the man had not been on the booze but still eyed him up warily. Phil in turn went over to her ladyship, apologising profusely to her, but she waved him away accepting it as she went off to the kitchen to fetch a glass of water. Jack was not happy though and neither was his Lordship.

"Listen here Phil," said Jack, "I won't have any of this nonsense. We have enough to do here without talk of ghosts. You hear me? Now get your act together, I don't pay you to lark about. It's almost time to finish up for the day, so get off home and clear your head, then see me here tomorrow morning."

Phil bowed his head knowing that work was hard to come by at the moment, but he knew what he'd seen and felt, nothing could sway him from the fact that Grasceby Manor was haunted. As he walked away Jack motioned to Lord Grasceby and asked if he could have a word with him alone. As they entered the Study he sent Simon upstairs to work with John, his carpenter, so he would be out of the way. Alone, he turned to his lordship.

"Tell me straight. Are there any ghostly things you haven't told me about?"

His lordship shook his head. "No, never seen or heard anything at all here and the staff have never said anything about such things. I'm sure they would have told me if they had. Your man did look quite frightened and he did ask me about a boy a couple of days back but I just shrugged it off." His lordship's expression became serious. "This isn't going to affect the schedule is it? I have to be ready for the opening in July you know, we've already gone to great lengths to promote it as a new attraction for the county. With last year's discovery of the original manor ruins nearby, I have high hopes for the future."

Jack smiled a little bitterly. "I will have words with him. Phil is normally a steadfast bloke but he has got a bit of family pressure so to speak, so perhaps that's the problem. Leave it with me sir, I'll make sure things stay on track." Jack left his lordship and headed outside to have words with Phil privately, but Phil had taken him literally at his word and already left.

Unfortunately he had not taken himself off home but gone straight to the Star and Crescent Moon Inn on the outskirts of Graseby. The owner, Marcus, poured another tot of whiskey for Phil as he listened to him whining on about a ghost boy at the manor. Neither realising that within earshot was a local radio news reporter eavesdropping and eagerly tapping away on her smart phone…

#

Secrets of Grasceby Manor

1864

George didn't really understand what was happening, but it seemed to concern the servants and if he'd heard right, his mother. The noise downstairs varied in intensity as someone (his father?) raised his voice then seemed to break down into what sounded like sobbing.

George turned over in his bed and hid under the sheets frightened to look out as it didn't sound nice at all. Muffled sounds suggested someone was coming upstairs and as they reached his room, he held his breath waiting for the door to open. Instead the muffled sound of footsteps on the thin carpet stopped outside his door.

They paused for a moment or two.

He took another deep breath and held it.

Then they moved away, he couldn't tell if it was to go back downstairs again or head up to the servant's quarters. He listened intently again but didn't realise how tired he was from the day playing in the garden and his eyelids drooped ever closer until he finally fell asleep.

Morning. His favourite of the servants, Annie, came into the room after tapping on the door and brought him his breakfast. She appeared oddly quiet but at the same time seemed to want to tell him something, but couldn't. She helped George get dressed but for some reason he had to put on his finest garments as if they were going to church.

Odd that, because they did that on Sundays and other special days like Christmas but today was, he looked at his fingers and quickly counted, Thursday!

He was getting good at this. He'd have to tell his mother as she'd be so proud. He then ate his breakfast like a good boy should do, so that he would grow up big and strong like his father.

Annie kept looking at him and he thought at one point she was going to burst into tears and a feeling of foreboding began to creep over George. She asked him if he was ready and he nodded. He liked Annie, she was like a big sister to him, she was kind and he loved to be cuddled by her. Especially when he was frightened or upset and she pulled him close to her. It was almost as good as when his mother did the same when she was at home.

He thought about Mother. He knew that she loved poetry and knew someone famous. His father would take her down to another place, perhaps near his uncle, where she would stay with that person learning about poetry, phil, philyosy, something odd sounding anyway and even learning something called Latin. She'd started teaching him this 'Latin' lately but he didn't know why and struggled to understand it.

Annie motioned for him to come with her and they left his bedroom. He was a very lucky boy. He had a very large room at the end of the second floor and off from it was his favourite room of all, his toy room.

Stuffed with everything you could imagine from a, too large really for him, rocking horse to a raggedy clown doll that apparently had belonged to his grandmother a long, long time ago, whenever that was.

He stopped letting his mind wander as Annie led him downstairs and into the big room with large windows in it and lots of light. It was his father's study and there he was sitting in his favourite chair.

George knew immediately something was wrong. His father looked worn out and was not as tidy as George knew he normally was. His father was a proud man and kept a very clean, tidy aspect so this was very odd indeed. Annie curtsied, left George standing in front of his father and hurried out of the room. He was sure he heard her start sobbing as she retreated into the distance and the feeling of foreboding returned.

"My dear, dear George, come to your father for I have some sad news to impart to you." His father beckoned to him and George obeyed and stood in front of his father with his hands clasped in front of him as he had been taught. "Come sit on my knee and promise me you will be a brave boy indeed." George nodded, meekly climbed upon his father's knee and waited quietly as his father appeared to compose himself. "George, I regret to tell you that Momma will not be coming home ever again."

His father paused to let this sink in, but George's puzzled face caused him to continue. "Your mother, my wife, was taken very ill a few days ago and she has now joined the heavenly angels where I'm sure she will watch over you and me. If you remember your lessons about heaven and where people go when they..." he hesitated and composed himself trying not to show George the pain he himself was suffering upon receiving the awful news late the previous evening. "...when they pass away.

I hope you will understand how much we are both going to miss her."

"B... but Father, why did she leave us? Did I do something wrong to upset her?"

"No son, you could never do anything to upset her. It was beyond our control and sadly these things do happen, even to very good people such as your mother. Now I need you to be a strong boy and not show the servants you are upset. We must be brave, my son, especially when we have to go to the church to bury her in a few day's time. Run along now, and remember, be strong for the memory of your mother."

George slipped off his fathers knee and turned to face him. "Can I go and visit mother in heaven father? Then we can be together again and she can tell me more of that 'philisology' thing she wanted me to learn."

His father looked pained but tried to smile at the innocence of his son. "No George, we never visit heaven until we're called for and I do hope we won't be called for a very long time."

George tilted his head as if to say something else but changed his mind. "Oh, OK father. Can I play in my room now?"

"Yes, yes of course. Then tomorrow young man, we will start again with your studies. It is what your mother would have wanted."

George smiled and rushed out of the room. It would be a few days before the reality that he would never see his mother again would finally sink in when he had to attend his mother's funeral. He was grateful that Annie could be with him as the tears flowed freely down his cheeks…

3: A second encounter

James was pleased. Everything was going well and the company he worked for had even surprised everyone with a bonus. 'Shock, horror, wonders will never cease', he thought and smiled to himself. Well they had after all secured a large contract to maintain the office computer systems and data services for a major, national no less, online retailer so they had certainly earned it.

Sally had been away at a police conference all week concerning 'forensic analysis of DNA sampling methods', which she said was fascinating but not as detailed as she'd have liked it to have been. Now she was back. It was the weekend and he smiled at that thought. Although she had not moved in with him, she did spend most weekends at his place, much to both of their delight.

Time to relax as they settled down to an evening to catch up and watch telly and probably an online movie or two. As Sally flicked through the channels as she often did, a semi familiar image flashed up before she passed on to the next. She stopped and slowly backed up the channels whilst James lay on the sofa half asleep and not paying much attention to the screen.

"Hey James, look at this?" She called to him and he stirred as Sally turned up the volume. The view was indeed familiar, it was the outside of Grasceby Manor and it was a local news bulletin.

"...since the recent renovations began, workmen have stated they've seen a small boy wandering the manor.

A spokesperson for the owners simply said they had no comment about the alleged ghost and that they did not believe in such things. Controversially, Lord Grasceby also seemed to imply that the workmen were looking for any excuse to explain their slow progress.

This is something that Jack Hammonds of 'Hammonds Restoration and Refurbishment' handling the renovations has strenuously denied. Hence the current stand off with all work stopping temporarily until his lordship has apologised. Grasceby Manor is being refurbished ready for the tourist season as, for the first time in its history, parts of it will be opened to the public, although planning delays mean this is now scheduled for sometime in July.

The owners' belief is that the income generated may help with the spiralling costs of maintaining such a property and its associated estate, so having the building works completed on time is of the utmost importance to them. Hence the current delay is causing the owners somewhat of a headache. I'm Emma Frasier, back to you, Patrick in the studio."

The view changed to the newsreader in the studio but he moved on to another story as Sally looked at James strangely. She muted the TV sound.

"Remember some weeks ago after Mike's funeral, didn't we meet an odd chap who mentioned something about a boy and the Manor?"

James shrugged his shoulders. "Well I wouldn't put it past them to try a publicity stunt. If that was the case then they did at least dress him up to play the part well. Perhaps he had been the first of their attempts to get publicity by sowing the seeds of a ghostly tale – only it didn't work with us, did it love?"

He smiled and he settled down and dozed off again. Sally channel hopped then came across one of her favourites, the final half of a romantic movie, yet another repeat of 'Love Actually'. However, as James dozed she couldn't help thinking back to their encounter with the Victorian looking gentleman. After a few minutes she finally picked up her smart tablet and went online.

#

"You awake love?"

Startled, James came to and started thinking to himself well I am now… as his eyes came to focus on Sally's face.

He was still on the sofa but the TV was off and he noted the time was almost eleven twenty pm. Damn, he thought, probably won't sleep now, but Sally was trying to get his attention.

"Something I remembered from the other week, you know, about that gentleman, we saw." James looked at her blankly and she continued, "The one who was asking about you seeing ghosts, remember?"

James sat up and then it came back to him. "So, what of it?" He said sleepily. Sally lifted the tablet computer up to him and showed him the screen.

He read the main text out loud.

"Horncastle Players put on the farce 'It ain't showbiz' and for this reviewer it hit the right spot in combining a modern..."

James shook his head, bewildered. "Sally I don't get it, what are you on about?"

She looked frustrated at him. "I guess it's my training as a detective, but something didn't seem right about the gentleman. We both commented on his attire, he really looked Victorian so I'd said to you he was probably involved in the local amateur dramatics' productions, perhaps over in Horncastle. Might have needed to come to the church for something, perhaps a prop and didn't have time to change, you get the picture."

James still looked puzzled so she continued. "But it says here they're doing a MODERN farce and there's no one acting as a Victorian gentleman in it. Not only that but I can't find any local am dram production dealing with that sort of era requiring that sort of character."

James had a blank stare on his face and shrugged. "So?"

"So who is he? And what was he doing dressed like that at Grasceby church?" Sally looked at him as if expecting an answer but James just shook his head.

"I don't know love but for now I don't think we really need to worry about it. Probably a coincidence and as I said earlier, perhaps it's all a big con to get tourists to visit Grasceby Manor.

Those sort of places need a lot of upkeep and they might be trying to lure the tourists in. Come on, let's be off to bed, it's getting late and to be honest I'm not bothered about ghosts any more. I've not seen Jenny or my parent's since they were reunited, nothing at all for months now so I'd rather just let things be and get on with life." He pulled her gently to him and kissed her on the lips. "Especially now I've got you in it." She smiled at him and stepped back with her arms on her hips and tilted her head to one side.

"Okay then, but humour me in the morning, let's just go down to your parents graves and if he doesn't turn up again then I'll forget all about it. Now, glass of wine before bed?" James nodded and Sally headed off to the kitchen to get the bottle and glasses.

#

"Groundsman's doing a good job I see." James looked round the three gravestones and inspected them carefully. They'd ended up coming over after lunch and now Sally was looking round the graveyard but it was as empty as the bench just up along the path. She sighed.

"We've been here half an hour now and I'm starting to feel foolish. Why didn't you shut me up about it this morning when we got up?"

James looked over to her and smiled. For someone who had been quite sceptical about ghostly goings on, Sally seemed to have come round to at least partially accepting he'd seen, not just his sister, but also his parents, sadly as ghosts.

He hadn't forgotten the day they'd gone back to 'Wolds View' cottage then on to visit Jenny's and Jack's grave shortly after Jenny had been buried next to her (and his, it transpired) father. It had also been the day he and Sally had discovered the truth about his family and especially his Mother. They'd gone to the cottage and after a short while as Sally sat in the car, James had seen all three of his former family appear briefly. It was as if they were saying thank you and it later came to light that as Sally had turned back to look at the cottage she had just caught a glimpse of three human figures just as they vanished.

She hadn't admitted it at the time but a few days later she came clean and accepted that there had been something odd. She wasn't fully convinced, trick of the light and all that, but she definitely seemed more open to the notion of ghosts than she had originally been, especially for a Detective Superintendent. Not that she'd admit it in public, she had to be seen to be scientific and sceptical about such things when it came to her police work.

Sally spotted the vicar just going into the church, so she indicated to James that she was going to speak to her and headed off along the path to catch up with the Reverend Cossant. She couldn't help thinking that it had to be a strain on the reverend having to cover several parishes, but she guessed that was a sign of the times.

James bent down to pluck a weed from next to Jenny's headstone. He wished he'd had a proper chance to know his sister and silently cursed what had happened all those years ago before he was even born.

He felt a momentary tingle and for a brief second could have sworn he heard Jenny saying 'speak to him'. He stood up shaking his head and turned to go up the path to join Sally when he spotted the Victorian gentleman sitting on the bench. He blinked and thought for a moment that Sally must have seen him as she walked along the path to the church. So why hadn't she come back to tell him so they could speak with the chap?

"Good day to you again, sir."

The gentleman stood up, took off his top hat, bowed slightly at James who found himself instinctively bowing back.

"How did you…" James voice trailed off then he found it again. "Look, I'm a patient man but you'd better explain yourself. Sneaking up on people like this. My partner is a Detective Superintendent you know and she'll soon be back." He looked round and over to the church entrance but Sally didn't appear. Seemed like James wasn't telepathic after all.

"I do apologise but you see I don't have a lot of control over this and frankly it is quite wearisome. May I ask if you have reconsidered my request as you have come back?"

James looked at him for a moment or two trying to decide if this was all a joke or a bad dream. "What? Oh, your missing nephew?"

James thought back and remembered the news report the previous night and also remembered what he'd thought of the gentleman in front of him.

"Look I don't mean to be rude but I think I've sussed your little scheme here.

Good try, but I think if the manor wants some publicity they really ought to simply get their act together and run adverts rather than all this play acting."

The gentleman looked pained but seemed to understand and slowly approached James. "I suspect dear sir, you haven't quite grasped the situation presented to you and I apologise for that, but I didn't want to... let's say, frighten you off."

James felt exasperation rise inside and he shook his head. "Look, games over, I'm going to ask you VERY nicely simply not to bother me or Sally again when we come to visit my family's graves, understand?" The gentleman placed his top hat back on his head with a sad and resigned look about him.

"Very well sir, you have my sincere apologies and I bid you farewell." With that the gentleman turned and walked away.

James shook his head and looked back towards his family's grave as a wave of coldness seemed to pass through him. He had suspected that at some stage it would become common knowledge that he'd seen his sister's ghost but didn't think it would happen so soon with people bugging him for help like this.

He turned back to size up the gentleman and try to memorise features so as to avoid him in the future but instead there was Sally walking back along the path to him.

"Well that was a waste of time, the Vicar knows nothing about our chappie and hasn't seen anything unusual lately."

James looked at her, a bemused and somewhat puzzled expression on his face.

"But you must have just walked past him, he was just here a moment ago talking to me!" James pointed back up along the path but Sally looked at him blankly and shook her head.

"Not seen anyone else except the Vicar and you." She looked quizzically at him. "Now don't you go telling me he's a blooming ghost as well. Remember I don't see things like that and as I've seen him then he has to be real. Don't you start flipping out on me Mr Hansone…" She sidled up to him and looked him in the eyes with a mischievous air about her. "Or I might just have to take you down to the station for questioning." She winked at him and James smiled.

'Time to go home' he thought and before he had a chance to say anything Sally, who had been thinking the same, grabbed him by the hand and led him back towards where they'd parked the car.

#

1864

George knew that Annie was looking for him. She'd been instructed to take him into the garden and explore the maze but being quite small for his age he had found little hollows and gaps at the roots of the hedges. He could cheat and crawl through between the hedge gaps and surprise Annie!

He heard her call his name, it seemed she was a long way off and he sniggered, only to be grabbed from the other side of the hedge and tickled.

She'd got him!

He laughed and crawled through to her and she gave him a cuddle then brushed off some of the specks of dirt and old leaves that clung to his clothes.

Annie was pleased that George was at last smiling after he'd finally realised his mother was never coming back. It had been like a sledgehammer to him when the truth dawned that awful day. Despite his promise to his father, George had broken down and sobbed into Annie's bosom, she too had caved in and joined him. Such had been the popularity of George's mother with the servants and for Annie especially in light of how they had taken her in and helped bring her up, even though she was of a lower class.

Annie smiled back, glad that George seemed to at last be getting back to his old, slightly mischievous, self. She led him by the hand along a section of the maze that she knew would lead back to the entrance when suddenly she heard a shriek and then wailing coming from the direction of the manor. She stopped in her tracks and George came to a halt beside her as he cocked his head to one side and listened to the noise. Annie blinked a couple of times as she listened and then realised something.

"That's Cooksie, Mrs Bottomly. Oh whatever's got into her and upset her like that?" Annie turned to George. "Come on master George, we'd better get ourselves back to the house and see what has got Cooksie all worked up."

George took that as a challenge and shot ahead of her before she had a chance to tell him to stay by her side.

She bolted after him trying to hold her skirt so that it didn't cause her to fall flat on her face. They reached the back entrance and Annie grabbed George, bringing him to a halt before he could rush in. After tidying him up she brushed herself down and straightened her own clothes before they proceeded through the back entrance and into the kitchen. No one was there and then they heard their names being called out.

It sounded like it was coming from the study so she took George by the hand and they passed through the kitchen into the hallway, approaching the door to the study. It was open and there seemed to be several people inside.

Entering, it was apparent that the servants had been gathered together along with Dr Frederickson and two people, a man and a woman, that Annie had seen visiting the household on several occasions, who she recognised as friends of his lordship. Dr Frederickson saw them enter and motioned for George to come to him and Annie to join the line of servants.

She indicated to George to go to the doctor then spotted Mrs Bottomly, whose tear stained face did not bode well. Very little upset the cook as she was built to withstand anything, or at least that's what Annie had always thought ever since her earliest memory of Grasceby Manor.

She quickly looked round the room but one person was missing. His lordship, but she knew he was away on business.

Dr Frederickson coughed loudly to get everyone's attention. "I have gathered you all here to share some terrible news with you.

Although I probably shouldn't have told Mrs Bottomly first as you know by now that something awful has happened. I have been informed this morning that your master, Mr Ferrymore, Lord Grasceby, was thrown from his horse whilst on the way to Dover and sadly was killed as a result.

The horse first threw him then it would appear fell against him, crushing him, there was nothing anyone could have done. It occurred in Grantham and I have arranged for Lord Grasceby's body to be brought here as soon as possible."

George was looking round at everyone as he tried to understand what the good doctor had just said. Deep inside he knew that this person Mr Ferrymore was something to do with him and he racked his brain trying to understand why everyone was so upset. Annie was looking at him with tears in her eyes and a brief flash of memory drifted across Georges' mind. Something he remembered his mother once said.

They were the lord and lady of the manor, Grasceby Manor. His name was Master George Hamilton Ferrymore, Ferrymore … The puzzled expression on George's face must have caught the doctor's attention, at the same time as he saw Annie trying to indicate to him something about George. He looked down just in time for George to tug on his trouser leg to get his attention.

"Doctor, isn't father the lord here?" The quiet voice asked.

Dr Frederickson looked down at the young boy, then got down onto one knee and faced George at his level.

"Yes George, I'm sorry to say they are one and the same. It is your father who has been tragically killed. I am so sorry to bring you this terrible news." George let this sink in and as the gravity of it dawned on him, he started shaking and his lips began to tremble.

"Bu.. Bu.. Does this mean father will be like mother and I'll not see him ever again? Not ever?"

The doctor nodded slowly and George burst into tears and looking round there was only one person he wanted to be with now. He rushed over to Annie and buried his head in her lap. She looked up at the doctor, in tears herself.

"Miss Annie please take Master George up to his room and console him for me, thank you."

She helped George and led him away as his crying became louder. The rest of the servants including Mrs Bottomly and the two people the doctor had brought with him watched them leave in stunned silence with an air of foreboding hanging over the room like a heavy cloud.

They turned to face the doctor with apprehension written on their faces as he began informing them of what would become of the manor. He turned to the couple indicating to them as he introduced Mr & Mrs Cording to the servants as caretakers of the manor and estates until George came of age.

4: Down tools again everyone!

John, the carpenter, studied the plans over and over again but as he looked at the panelled walls, he could not quite get them to match the plans he'd been given. They'd all returned to work again after reassurances that there was no ghost boy at the manor, John was one of those who had been pretty annoyed at the break in the work schedule – for some stupid ghost. He had no time for such nonsense and was annoyed with Phil, his colleague, when he went public about seeing a ghostly boy in the kitchen and in the basement.

In a desperate attempt to get things back on track, Lord Grasceby had reluctantly called in a ghost hunter. After several days roaming around the manor, he duly declared that, apart from a ghostly cat, he could not sense nor find any human ghost in the building. It was most probably the ghostly cat that had spooked some of the workers. Despite a few grumblings, mainly from Phil, who insisted he'd seen a boy and not a cat, work restarted on refurbishing the interior décor and the wooden wall panelling that adorned many of the rooms, at great expense.

Odd style really, he thought, but a couple of generations back, the owners had been known to be somewhat eccentric and always did things their own way rather than follow fashion. Apparently, nobody had told them at the time that they were out of date and behind the times.

John shook his head again and turned to call the works' supervisor but as he shivered suddenly for no reason, he thought he caught movement out of the corner of his left eye and turned back to look down the hallway.

Nothing.

"Damned imagination, now they've got me seeing things", he grumbled and fished his smart phone out to call his boss. He briefly smiled at the phone's wallpaper cover image of a Lancaster in flight. He pressed the contacts icon, quickly found the number and activated it.

"Hi Jack, I'm in the hallway on the second floor, yes, you know the long one with the store rooms branching off it and the library at the end? I can't make head nor sense of the plans you gave me. Can you just pop up and take a look. Ta, will do, see you in a minute." He put the phone back into his pocket and heard something shuffle on the floor behind him. Turning quickly, he spooked the lord's tabby cat 'Mr Shabernackles' who shot past him hissing as it did so.

John shook his head as he watched the cat race for the stairs and disappear down out of view. "That's the bloody ghost if you ask me. Stupid name for a cat, 'Shabernackles', what the hell was he thinking? Never heard such a daft name in all my years."

A little voice behind him made him jump out of his skin and he spun round.

"I named him and he's MY cat, so there!" said the lord's nine year old daughter, Heather, as she stormed off after the cat.

John shook his head again wondering what the world was coming to. He turned round as he looked at his watch wondering where Jack had got to, only to see the boy standing looking at him oddly. John frowned as he hadn't heard anyone else walk along the wooden floor of the hallway, heaven knows it creaked like nobody's business, but his job here was to check over the wall panelling, not the floor.

The boy turned and without a word, walked away from him down the hallway towards the largest room on this floor, the library. Instead of heading for the door however, he walked through the wall and out of sight. John blinked, stared for a few moments open mouthed, he did not hear Jack come up the stairs, so naturally he was startled when his boss spoke.

"Let's see the plans then as I haven't got all day. Blooming kid and that damned cat near enough tripped me coming up the stairs." John didn't answer as he was still staring at the far end wall. Jack peered round him and yet again John was startled.

"Err, sorry, what was that again?" He stammered.

Jack looked suspiciously at his best, and had to be admitted, only, carpenter and again peered round him towards where he'd been staring. "DON'T frigging tell me... now you've seen something?" Jack looked accusingly at John.

"No, no, of course not – I was just, you know, wondering about the extent of the panelling along here.", he lied. His white face told a different story.

"Now look John, we've got a big job on here and I can't afford any more stupid delays, so tell me I can rely on you not to say anything – yes I can tell something's up, you've got a face whiter than the bloody ceiling artex! Whatever you've seen, keep it to yerself, got it?"

John nodded.

"Good. That's settled then. Now what about these plans?"

John brought a smart tablet out of his bag on the floor next to his feet and pointed out several discrepancies in the panelling but realised it was probably nothing and didn't really affect what he was supposed to be doing. Jack looked over the plans then along the walls either side of the hallway.

"Well as far as I'm concerned, I don't care that there's more panels than we'd been led to believe. Our job is simply to replace those that are falling apart so just measure those up, take pics for comparison purposes and get it done as quick as you can."

Jack looked at John sternly then turned and walked back to the stairs muttering under his breath as he did so. He quickly disappeared out of sight and John turned back facing towards the far end of the hallway. Plucking up courage, he strode down it and stood next to the wall, tapping all along it until he came to the door at the right-hand side, but everything seemed in order.

Opening the door he looked tentatively inside. The library was a long room filled with several large bookcases chock-a-block with books of every conceivable size, thickness and weight. Standing on the other side of the wall from the hallway were bookcases that would take several people to move, even with the books removed.

He shook his head and went back to work in the hallway without noticing the boy looking out the window at the far side of the room.

#

"Hey, Phil, come and look at this that Heather's got." Simon motioned to Phil who walked across the room to stand next to him and Heather. He looked down at her smart tablet and wondered what the world was coming to when nine-year olds spent more time on social networking sites than actually talking to their school friends in real life. Heather had caught up with her cat as it reached the downstairs study-cum-living room. It was also part of the renovations and he and Simon were supposed to be finishing off the right-hand wall. Mr Shabernackles was purring merrily away as Heather carried him to look out the window, whilst Simon showed Phil the latest silly cat video to be uploaded.

Phil looked at it and pressed play once again and did chuckle as the cat on a skateboard did its tricks. Mind you Jack would be furious if he knew they weren't working at the moment, allowing themselves to be distracted. Heather did like showing them what she'd found on the latest sites and it certainly relieved the stress of the last week.

Anyhow – back to work, he decided – especially as their boss had left them and gone upstairs to see the carpenter, John, about something or other. Jack Hammonds was not someone to get on the wrong side of. He wasn't happy with Phil and had nearly sacked him after he claimed he'd seen the ghost of the boy. How was he to know, that the lass sitting on the next table at the Star and Crescent Moon Inn was a radio newshound?

News coverage the other week certainly hadn't helped matters. If he'd known a news reporter was eavesdropping, he'd have never said a word. He looked down and realised they needed the water bucket filling up and the bag of plaster was almost out as well. "Hey up Simon, gi'us a hand and stop faffing about now – we'd best be getting on. Heather luv, can you take yer cat out now and let us get on please?"

Heather looked at him and tilted her head to one side whilst cradling Mr Shabernackles in her arms. "Oh, you're no fun today anyway and I don't think Mr Shabernackles likes you anymore." She turned to look back out of the bay window and Phil motioned to Simon to pick up the bucket, and to follow him out of the room. Simon scampered after him as he passed out into the hallway, the young apprentice keen to do as he was told.

Phil felt the chill as he walked through and into the kitchen so that he could fill the bucket whilst Simon popped out to the van to get a new bag of plaster. He hummed quietly to himself whilst looking across at the gardens, heard the van door slam shut and smiled to himself. Simon was quite keen, but did have a habit of slamming doors instead of closing them properly. An impetuous youth he was indeed, but to be fair, a good 'un and someone quite dependable.

Bucket filled, he turned and walked through the partially open kitchen door, pushing it with his elbow. As he passed into the hallway, he saw Simon come in through the front entrance door then stop suddenly, open mouthed. Phil started to turn to look in the same direction as Simon but suddenly a black and white figure passed through him from the bottom of the stairs and into the kitchen, as an icy sensation come over him then just as rapidly faded away.

He dropped the bucket.

Water gushed across the stone hallway as he blinked and wiped his eyes in disbelief then turned back to Simon.

"You... you saw that... right? Tell me you SAW THAT?" He stammered and pointed towards the kitchen. Simon was white as a sheet, put the bag of plaster down, walked up to Phil, passed him and went into the kitchen peering carefully round the door. He shook his head but then noticed their boss coming down the stairs.

"What are you two skivers up to then eh?" Jack said, but then noticed the water on the floor. "WHAT THE HELL HAVE YOU DONE?" Then he noticed the white faces on both his workers. "OK, don't you DARE tell me something else has happened!"

Phil looked up at his boss but was now angry.

"I don't care what you are paying me – I'm not staying here until someone figures out what the hell is going on!"

With that Phil stormed out of the hallway and out into the grounds of the manor. Jack looked shocked at how Phil had responded and turned to Simon who was now clearly shaken and upset.

"I'm, I'm sorry Mr Hammonds, but a girl, a servant like person, just came down the stairs before you and walked right through Phil and into the kitchen – fair freaked him and me out. 'Tis the truth boss, honest it is."

Simon waited for Jack to go into a rage but Jack had seen the looks on their faces for himself and he knew it was the same as John upstairs. Before he could say anything, Lord Grasceby came through the front entrance with a puzzled look about his face.

"Hammonds, what the hell is the matter with your plasterer outside. He absolutely refuses to step into the building and is talking about going home and not coming back! I do hope we're not going to have anymore trouble like the other week, absolutely ridiculous! It's about time you employed someone decent and not time wasters like that."

Jack had heard enough now and walked up to and stood right in the face of Lord Grasceby.

"Now that's ENOUGH about my lads. All three of them have seen something strange in the last few minutes or so and I for one have had enough. I may not believe in anything out of the ordinary, but I've seen their faces this time for myself and I believe all of them have witnessed something peculiar here. Until you get to the bottom of this, we're finished here – I don't even care if you get someone else in to finish the job do ya hear me?"

Lord Grasceby stood back abashed at this outburst, lost for words. Jack got his phone out and speed dialled his carpenter upstairs.

"John, collect your tools NOW and meet me at the van. No, no you haven't done anything wrong, just meet me outside, OK?" He turned to Simon and motioned to him to leave. Simon hesitated then thought better than to question why, realising his boss was not in the mood. He hurriedly grabbed his coat from the study and dashed out past Jack whilst Lord Grasceby glared at Jack.

"Listen Hammonds, if you drop me in it now, then I'll sue you for breaking your contract and not finishing the job you started, so help me I will. We've only got a couple more months left until we're supposed to open, you know – damned if I'll be forced to delay that after all our preparations."

Jack turned to Lord Grasceby and from his expression, it was clear he didn't care a jot.

"Then it's up to you isn't it? Sort this ghost thing out – something's happened here to bring it or them out after all these years. I thought that 'so called' ghost hunter said it was just a ghost cat – my men have seen a little boy and now today a bloody servant wench – they're no sodding cat if you ask me."

He paused as if something had flickered into his mind just as John came down the stairs looking apprehensive. He didn't stop to ask his boss what the fuss was about and rushed outside to join his colleagues. He knew he had an apology to give to Phil as well!

Jack faced his lordship again.

"There's that chap – rumour says he was actually the one who solved that missing girl's case last year. Rumour also has it he's supposed to have seen her ghost and it led him to where she was buried. I don't know how true that is but if you really want me and my men to finish this job then find out what happened here! James – something or other – can't remember his surname, but I'd bet someone down at the inn will know. Until you do, I don't want to hear from you, except with the payment for what work we've already done. Goodbye!"

With that, Jack walked out to join his men who were still stood next to the van not knowing what to make of events. Lord Grasceby stood dumbfounded and could only look round at the sorry state of the very wet tiled floor of the hallway, scratching his head in dismay.

#

1864

It had been nearly six weeks since his father's funeral and according to Annie, George had been a very strong boy and made her proud by not crying. His only uncle, Lord Silverwright, who was his mother's brother, lived a long way away so the lord had not seen him much since George had been born. Lord Silverwright had overseen the funeral arrangements and had arranged for the house to be looked after by Mr & Mrs Cording on the recommendation of the good Doctor Frederickson. They were a less well off couple of noble birth who had been friends of Lord and Lady Ferrymore for several years, even before George had been born.

Annie didn't like them.

They were to take up residence in the manor to be stepparents to George and oversee his growing up. Once he was of age, he would then take up his inheritance on the condition that he would always look after his stepparents and ensure they had somewhere to live, as grateful thanks for looking after him. The servants would be kept on as long as there was sufficient income from the various estates that the Ferrymores controlled, so at least for the time being the future of the manor and George was assured.

Mr & Mrs Cording appeared kind enough and for the first few weeks George began to settle down to a routine not too different from what he'd been used to. He had a tutor come in three days of the week to give him schooling since his mother's passing and with Annie often being given charge to look after him at other times to make sure he had his meals, life seemed to settle down.

That is until the tutoring stopped three months later. One morning, Mr Cording called George into the study and sat him down. He explained that the cost of hiring the tutor was too much at a time when the estates were not making enough. Mrs Cording would help with his schooling from now on and he was to pay attention to her and be a good boy. George was sad, as Mrs Harmon had been nice to him and very understanding when he didn't quite understand something. Still he was sure Mrs Cording would also be good to him.

He was wrong.

Almost from the first lesson, it was clear that Mrs Cording did not have a fraction of the patience of either Mrs Harmon or Annie, very soon he began to dread the upcoming lessons.

Today was no exception. He was led down to the study with Annie trying to reassure him everything would be OK. He stepped into the room and there she was, the horrible woman, Mrs Cording. She motioned to him to sit where she indicated, she opened out a large sheet showing a map of the world.

"Today you are going to tell me the name of each of the countries I point to and you will get it right, understand? You know what will happen if you get any wrong. We've been over this map several times and over several days so you should by now know them off by heart." She pointed at a place on the map and he hesitated...

"Egypt?"

Mrs Cording looked disappointed but nodded to say he'd got it right. He was thrilled and thought perhaps today would be better after all. She pointed to another place and he looked.

"India."

She grunted satisfaction again so moved her finger around the map until she suddenly stopped and motioned for him to identify another country. George hesitated this time as it was quite tiny. "Africa?" He offered and for a second he thought Mrs Cording would explode!

"No, no, stupid, it's Malta, Africa is a continent!"

This went on for some time and George became exasperated, until finally Mrs Cording sent him away to his room. She was in a bad mood and there was nothing George could have done to have improved it.

Over the following days it seemed to George that he couldn't get anything right for her. She seemed to get more angry with each passing lesson until one day Mrs Cording suddenly snapped and smacked him across the back of the legs.

George burst into tears and tried to rush away but she was having none of it and grabbed him by the arm.

"Now you listen here you little whelp, I'm in charge and we'll have none of these tantrums now I'm your tutor. You're lucky, if you ask me, to have me to teach you. Go to your room and DON'T say a word to the servants, especially that Annie – I've seen how you like to be near her. I'll put a stop to that I will, if you don't buckle down to yer studies."

George nodded frantically and rushed away from her as she released her grasp and he escaped to his room. Over the next three weeks his studies became harder and he received more smacks to the legs until he started to find it painful to walk. Annie asked him several times if he was all right and naturally he wanted to tell her but feared he would lose the only other person, other than his parents, who seemed to love him.

A couple of times instead of Mrs Cording, the lessons were taken by Mr Cording but he seemed just as severe as his wife and George began to wonder if he could ever escape them.

Gradually over the next couple of weeks he started to notice his meals were becoming plain and boring, not to mention there was less food each time. If he didn't know better, the Cordings, seemed to be trying to starve him!

Occasionally Annie and sometimes even Heather brought him extra bits of bread and meat which he scoffed down like a wolf but he knew they were taking a risk. Heather was always very quiet, she was at least good to him when she came to his room but he did prefer Annie's company when all was said and done.

He lay on his bed and began to cry into his pillow.

5: A chance encounter

It was a gorgeous late April morning and James decided that as he had the day off, he would take a drive out to Lincoln. Sally's birthday was coming up and despite lots of online shops tempting him to buy, he still liked to occasionally have a browse round real shops. Sally had, of course, been dropping a few subtle (or was that not so subtle?) hints about what she would really like. However, at this stage, a trip to Australia was out of the question although James had tried to worm a bit of extra holiday out of his boss and good friend, Mark. Mark had not been impressed however, so it was off to Lincoln to see what James could find, knowing full well that whatever he got was not a holiday 'down under'.

Lincoln city centre was busy, the weather had brought everyone out and parking was a struggle, not to mention a trifle expensive. It reminded him of when he used to live on the outskirts of London, although in those days he took the tube into work in the city. Memories of seeing the traffic jams as he passed by on the train back then, also reminded him why he had fallen in love with Lincolnshire. Despite still being quite rural in nature he loved the wide open spaces and views across the gently sloping countryside.

Looked at from certain parts of the A158 the scenery gave the impression of open space, although over in the Lincolnshire Wolds he knew there were several deep valleys, especially near Cadwell Park, Lincolnshire's motor racing circuit up between the town of Louth and his adopted town of Horncastle.

In another direction, Lincoln Cathedral stood proudly on Lincoln Edge, way off in the distance and could be seen from just outside Horncastle. Along with Boston's St Botolph's tall church tower locally known as 'The Stump' they were impressive landmarks of the county of Lincolnshire. A more recent addition also stood proudly just south of Lincoln, the memorial to the WWII Bomber Command and he realised he had yet to visit it. James and his ex wife, Helen, had managed to have a few drives out into the countryside before things turned sour in their relationship, but had not visited the memorial centre as it had still been under construction.

Now James was determined to see if Sally wanted to have a random drive out into the countryside on a nice day, although he knew she was a Lincolnshire lass born and bred, so perhaps she wouldn't be that bothered. It might be like teaching Granny to suck eggs, he thought and chuckled to himself.

He popped into the Lincoln Archives, being a member, he took a quick look through a variety of records. They now allowed people to save details and documents to a data stick, he found whatever he could on the modern Grasceby Manor and quickly stored it. James had been struck by an urge to look the Manor up after finally deciding upon Sally's present, a butterfly necklace with three small jewel encrusted gold butterflies he'd spotted in the jeweller's part way down Steep Hill.

He chuckled to himself, 'they certainly got that name right!' Remembering that he'd always been told Lincolnshire was flat.

No one had mentioned the Lincoln Edge with the Cathedral standing proudly at the top, let alone the gentle undulations of the Lincolnshire Wolds further towards the coast. He sat as he recovered from the steep walk back up the hill to the quaint bookshop near to the top just past the entrance to the castle. For a few moments he contemplated popping in for a book on Butterflies but decided against it in case Sally already had one.

It had only been the other week Sally had surprised him at the weekend when, on a sunny day, she'd rushed out into the garden and using her smart phone taken lots of pictures of a male Orange Tip butterfly. It transpired she was into lepidoptery, the study of butterflies and moths, James had smiled at this new discovery he'd made about her.

His mind had wandered. He finished saving the data and waved goodbye to Sheila on the desk who'd got used to him asking lots of questions. Helen his ex, had been the amateur genealogist. Now he was on his own, James had made a point of picking up just enough to start looking into his own family tree now he knew the truth about his family.

He blinked as he stepped outside, briefly lost in thought, wondering what Sally was up to at the moment. He almost stepped out into the road without looking, stopping himself just in time as a van whizzed by giving a sharp blast on its horn. For a brief moment he could have sworn an invisible hand had pushed him back onto the pavement just in time but he brushed away the thought and headed back towards the car park.

The journey back started off slowly due to the sheer volume of traffic but soon he was heading out on the main road and the traffic lessened. Approaching Wragby a sudden impulse found him taking a familiar road but one that he had not been on for a few months. He smiled and wondered if Jenny was guiding him as he realised that he would soon be at the small turn off for Grasceby. That brought back memories, both good and bad.

Sure enough, round the bend, the turning quickly appeared and without hesitation he took it, eager to see 'Wolds View' cottage again. The road twisted and turned and the ribbon of trees began as he remembered it before going past the old airfield.

Not long now he thought.

The tree line seemed to dip back on his left hand side and he slowed, taking care to check that no one was following close behind.

'Wolds View' cottage stood back from the road but James did a double take and slowed to a halt as he pulled onto the road side. A 'for sale' sign had a 'sold' sticker on it and deep inside James knew it would never be the same again. Whilst his original family home had been derelict he had held the hope that maybe he would one day buy the property and effectively return to his roots, but now the 'sold' sign put paid to that.

He let out a little sigh then wondered if it was worth calling in at the Star and Crescent Moon inn on the other side of the village to see if Marcus or Charles knew who had bought the property. He resolved to do just that and continued towards Grasceby.

As he passed the village pond on his right, the walls of the manor came into view on the left and he turned to look up at the upper floors of the manor. They were visible from the road and not hidden by the walls. The far righthand window caught his attention as he spied a boy looking out from it and James blinked a couple of times. The boy was still there. Must be the son of the owner, James decided, but on an impulse he slowed down, pulled onto the grass verge and stopped the car. He felt daft but something inside kept telling him it was important, and he sat there for a few moments in deep contemplation until suddenly a tap at his window made him jump...

"Whatcha doing?"

The little girl's voice startled him as he hadn't seen her come up to the car. Heather knew she shouldn't be outside the walls and indeed talking to a stranger but she had felt compelled to approach this person who'd parked up outside her home and was staring at it. She thought that was quite rude of the person and had decided to ask him what he was doing.

James regained his composure, wound down the window and smiled at her.

"Sitting here for the time being, and who may I ask are you?" Heather looked at the car, deep in thought, then turned and looked at James.

"I was always told not to speak to strangers but I've already done that so I guess it's OK now. I'm Heather and my father is the Lord of the Manor. You're not a thief are you, 'cos if you are then I'll have to scream and everybody will come running out here and get you."

James chuckled to himself at the thought, and her straightforward, to the point attitude. He briefly wondered if her father was like that.

"No Heather, I'm not a thief at all, now would a thief stay here knowing you might scream the place down? I think not. My name is James and I'm pleased to meet you. So what's your brother's name then?"

Heather looked at James as if he was out of his mind.

"I'm not daft, I don't have one of those, only Mr Shabernackles." James thought about asking who or what that was, but decided against asking the question.

"So who is the boy I just saw in the window over at your house, a visitor?" Heather looked round at the house then shrugged.

"Oh – THAT boy. He's nobody. Sometimes I see him and most of the time I don't. He comes and goes at any time really. Mr Shabernackles can't seem to decide if he is a nice boy or not as sometimes he hisses horribly when he's around and other times he's a nice pussy."

James took this in whilst scanning the front of the manor but the boy had gone. He knew deep inside that something almost inevitable was happening and a chill passed through him.

"How long have you seen this boy for then, Heather?" He enquired but noticed the look on her face. She was getting bored now and was swaying her body slightly from one side to the other.

She abruptly stopped mid sway.

"I'm fed up now, bye bye Mr James. Come along Mr Shabernackles."

James had not spotted the cat weaving its way round her feet whilst Heather was talking to him and she didn't wait for him to say anything but instead just walked off towards the manor's driveway and disappeared inside the open gates.

Mr Shabernackles sat down staring at James intently as James began to feel a chill in the air, suddenly the cat stood up, turned and rushed away to catch up with Heather.

"Well I'll be…", was all James could say and he once again looked over the manor for any sign of the boy but the windows remained empty. He shook his head, started the car and drove off, completely forgetting to call at the inn. He was preoccupied with thoughts about what the gentleman at Grasceby churchyard had mentioned.

About a young boy at the manor…

#

Marcus looked up to see Jack and his three workers enter the Star and Crescent Moon Inn. None of them looked happy and the youngest, his old friend Fred's grandson Simon, certainly seemed at a loss as if he didn't know why he was there. They took a table at the far end of the inn and as his own granddaughter, Sharon, started to head in their direction he held her back much to her surprise and annoyance. Perhaps that was because he knew she'd been seeing Simon on and off for the last few months.

However, he could tell something was troubling Jack. He couldn't remember a single time when he'd come in with all his workers.

Marcus casually walked over to them and stood next to Jack who looked up with a grimace on his face.

"Nowt for the time being Marcus, we've business to sort first." Marcus glared at Jack then relaxed and nodded.

"All right – but if you're still here in twenty minutes I'll expect an order – can't have folk taking up space if they're not supping or eating summat."

As Marcus walked back to the bar Jack turned and faced the other three. "I want you to describe as best you can what each of you saw, you first Phil."

Although he looked uncomfortable, Phil launched into describing his three encounters, two of the boy and the third of the servant. Simon backed Phil up with the servant as he had been the one to see her first as he returned through the front door. Then it was John's turn and he reluctantly related his encounter with the boy on the second floor of the manor.

Jack sat back, pondered what his colleagues had said and noted that Marcus was keeping an eye on them from the bar. He indicated to him for service, Marcus nodded and came over ready for their order.

But Jack had a different request to make.

#

1864

George came up with a plan. He knew he couldn't say anything to Annie as he dare not risk her being taken away from him.

But he also knew that the only other person that might help was the man whom his uncle also trusted, Dr Frederickson. So now it was late at night and as George stood naked by the wide open window he hoped that the terribly cold wind now hitting him would cause him to catch cold. He shivered as the cold biting wind seemed to slice through him and he gritted his teeth.

Even at his mere age of seven he knew it was risky but he had to get the doctors attention and the only way he would visit the manor was if someone was ill. That someone had to be George if he was to have any chance of speaking to the doctor about his fears.

He shivered violently again and was regretting standing there but he knew he had to do something. He shivered again and looked downwards. His father had called it his 'little dangler' but at the moment he wasn't sure he could even see it anymore! George wondered how long he should stay exposed like this but couldn't remember when he'd started, so reluctantly he decided to close the window and curtains. Gratefully he threw his nightgown back on and dived into bed burying himself deep under the sheets. Although it took a while he finally stopped shivering and fell into a deep but restless slumber.

It worked.

It was Heather, the other house maid who'd come to get him up and bring him his, by now, meagre breakfast. Instead she found George in a feverish state and quickly ran out of the bedroom to fetch Mrs Cording.

Annie heard the commotion but Mrs Cording gave her a withering look and told her to go to the kitchen to help Mrs Bottomly, the cook.

Reluctantly she did as she was told.

Upstairs Mrs Cording checked George's temperature and shook her head but inside however she was secretly pleased. Would speed things up if the little brat died now of natural causes instead of it being forced, she thought, all the while keeping her face straight and emotionless. She knew though they needed a little more time as the doctor was finalising the details with Lord Silverwright regarding the manor and it's estate if George should 'somehow' pass away unexpectedly like perhaps his mother. She resisted a grim smile to herself and went out of the room and downstairs to find the footman.

Less than an hour later Dr Frederickson arrived and was shown to George's room by Mrs Cording.

"Now master George, what is the matter with you?" he asked as he sat down at George's bedside and began to examine George. George explained he was cold and couldn't stop shivering and sneezing.

"Doctor, I'm not going to pass away like my mother am I?" he whimpered and Dr Frederickson held him by the wrist whilst he checked his pulse.

"No, I doubt it George, I doubt it very much. You have caught a cold, perhaps been outside a little too much have we?"

He turned to Mrs Cording. "I would recommend George should stay in his room for at least a week or perhaps two.

He should be given only hot broth with a few vegetables until he gets his strength back." He got up from the side of the bed but George grabbed his hand and held on to him.

"Don't go, not yet, please, I want to ask about mother", pleaded George as he let go. The doctor turned to Mrs Cording and nodded to her.

"I'll stay just a little while and settle him down. I'll see you in the study in a few minutes. Did you say Mr Cording was in Horncastle?"

Mrs Cording smiled and nodded at him, then left the room. George again grabbed the doctors hand.

"I need to tell you something. It's, it's, well.." Dr Frederickson looked impatiently at him.

"Spit it out boy!"

George took a deep breath.

"I don't like Mr & Mrs Cording, they're keeping me prisoner. They shout at me when I don't understand their lessons and they beat me if I get anything wrong. I think they are not feeding me properly now as well, as I don't get all my normal meals any more. I'm afraid. Can you tell uncle Arthur for me? I'm sure you and he can do something about them or even just ask them to be nice to me."

Dr Frederickson looked into George's eyes and for a moment George saw something in them that sent a chill down his spine.

Then the doctor smiled.

"Now, now George. You must not tell lies about people like that. They are only trying to help you and you have to try harder for them."

"Bu..but I'm not lying." George flung the bedclothes off and pulled up his nightgown to reveal the marks and bruises on his legs from the thrashings he'd been getting. Dr Frederickson looked at them carefully and shook his head.

"Oh dear, well I never, I'm so sorry George. This does change everything. I shall have words with Lord Silverwright as soon as I can as this is not right indeed. I am so sorry to have doubted you. You must promise me though to keep this quiet until I can get in touch with your uncle. Do you promise not to say anything, even to Annie?" George looked at him but just nodded in agreement.

Patting him on the head, Dr Frederickson stood up ready to leave. "Good boy, leave it to me and get back into bed now. I'll sort things out for you. Goodbye George and remember, not a word to anyone, anyone you understand..."

George nodded and pulled the bedclothes back over him and as he snuggled down he felt happy that at last something was going to be done.

Dr Frederickson walked downstairs with an angry look on his face. He walked into the study to find Mrs Cording waiting for him. She started to smile but saw his expression. He didn't wait for her to ask what was wrong.

"You blithering fools! What do you think you will gain if you strike the boy when we're not ready? He's just asked me to talk to his uncle and complained at the mistreatment you've been giving him. You are supposed to look after him until I've finished convincing Lord Silverwright to sign over the deeds of the estate into your hands if George falls ill and passes away before he's of age.

You've jeopardised everything just because you can't keep your temper under control!"

For once Mrs Cording cowered and tried to explain.

"But he's a brat and can't remember anything I've taught him. He doesn't deserve this place, we do!" She looked into the doctor's face trying to appeal to him. "I'll wager it's a bluff, his writing is poor and he can't get anything posted himself unless one of the servants helps him. Mind you that Annie might be a problem. He's as fond of that wench as if she's his sister and I'd bet she would try something if she thought he would come to harm."

Dr Frederickson took her by her arms and looked into her eyes.

"I have to see Lord Silverwright in two days. That's when I'm hoping he will sign the documents I've prepared. Once that's done then we need to allow a few more weeks, if not months before something can happen to the boy. Any sooner and his lordship may finally get off his backside and start taking an interest in what's happening here at the manor. We're just lucky he's away so often and doesn't pay much attention to what goes on up here."

He looked at her slyly. "When is your hapless husband due back today?"

Mrs Cording smiled.

"We have a few hours yet and the servants are either in the town with him getting supplies or otherwise very busy with chores and won't disturb us." The doctor's expression changed to a smile and he took her in his arms and began to kiss her.

Unbeknownst to them, Annie had arrived back early and was just about to enter when she'd heard the latter part of the conversation. Peeking through the partially opened door she saw them kissing passionately. She took a quick intake of breath and hurried away to the kitchen.

She knew what this meant.

The doctor was in collusion with Mrs Cording! And that didn't bode well for George.

6: A call and a letter

His phone suddenly beeped, disturbing James' concentration as he waded through the documents he'd saved from his visit to the archives in Lincoln. He was surprised to see from the display it was Marcus trying to call and he answered, intrigued.

"Hey up Marcus, you okay? Not often I get a call from you!"

He heard Marcus chuckle on the other end.

"Well considering you wanted to keep quiet about seeing ghosts it would seem a few more people seem to know your secret."

"How's that then?" James frowned.

"I've had Jack Hammonds, of Hammonds Restoration and Refurbishment pop in and ask a few questions, especially if I knew who you were and if it were true you'd seen ghosts locally. I played dumb and just said I'd heard rumours about a chap but didn't mention your name. After all you and I are the only living ones who saw your sister, even though neither of us knew who she was at the time. I've never told anyone about it, so where he got it from about you I don't know.

However, the thing is that one of his workers a few weeks back claimed he'd seen a ghostly boy wandering around the manor at Grasceby. You may have seen the hassle it caused as Phil was telling me all about it over a pint and a reporter had overheard him. Hence all the fuss on the TV and radio for a day or so. It just seems odd to have Phil's boss, Jack, now come in and ask about someone who can see ghosts. I wonder what's going on up at the manor?

Thought it might be of some interest to you just in case someone stops you in the street. Anyhow, I've done my bit. How's that there young lady of yours anyway?" he said, changing the subject.

James smiled.

"Oh, she's fine thanks, quite busy though, I got a message earlier saying she'd be late – sounds like there's been a hit and run up near Caistor and she's leading the investigation. Always something on our roads eh? Thanks for forewarning me, I'll be on the lookout for this Jack if he calls. See you soon. Cheers."

James heard Marcus say 'ciao' on the other end and hang up. He looked at the wall whilst focusing into the distance, pondering what Marcus had told him. Things were decidedly odd and too many little things seemed to be trying to push him into looking into this ghostly sighting of a boy. James didn't feel comfortable though, he was not a ghost hunter and it had been circumstances that had come together the last time. At least then he had a direct connection with Jenny even if he did not know it at the time. But he was troubled by seeing that boy in the window at the manor and the revelation that Heather did not have a brother but was aware of this boy nonetheless.

Intriguing. Troubling. But undoubtedly mysterious and indeed fascinating at the same time. Oh dear, he thought, it feels inevitable he would end up having to take a look.

James turned back to the information on his smart tablet that he'd got from Lincoln Archives but there wasn't really that much concerning Grasceby Manor.

There were a few bare bones bits such as roughly when and why it was built and that at one time the manor had changed hands from one family to another. He sat back after a while and decided to leave it for that evening. He put some music on before dropping off to sleep on the sofa.

#

Sally did indeed get to his place quite late and she was exhausted and not in the mood for ghosts, so James held off saying anything until the next day, fortunately it was a Saturday. She had to leave early though as she'd a couple of witnesses to the accident come forward and she was going to interview them that morning. James admired her work ethic but couldn't help feeling being in the force dictated her life.

It wasn't until around 2pm when she got back and was finally able to put her feet up that James could recount most of what had transpired the day before. Omitting of course details of her birthday present.

"Wonder who's been putting it about that you've seen ghosts? Certainly wasn't me!", she reflected as she polished off the sandwiches James had prepared. James sat down next to her and admired her legs for the umpteenth time.

"Sorry, what was that love? Oh, you know what, I bet it was Charles. Haven't seen him for a few months now but I reckon he suspected you know.

Remember he was one of the first to see me at Wolds View cottage and one night he realised I must have seen Jenny's ghost. You know, when it was foggy and I thought I'd run someone over. I was also with that scumbag Craig that night, so I don't really like to think about that part."

Sally nodded remembering that Craig and James' wife, Helen had eventually had an affair. However, on the plus side it had meant James had become free to see herself so it wasn't all bad in the end.

"Are you going to talk to Jack? I remember his dad, Harold, running the business before Jack took over the reins. If I remember right Jack is a very practical man and ghosts are not the sort of thing he would believe in. Mind you, I didn't expect to fall for someone who has paranormal tendencies so who am I to talk!"

James looked appreciatively at her and leaned over and brushed a few crumbs off her chin.

"And I'm mightily pleased you don't hold it against me." He smiled at her. "You know it is bugging me now and I do feel like I want to pop over to Grasceby churchyard to see if that chap is there again. I have a real funny feeling about all this now and I don't think I'm going to be able to let it go."

Sally knew where this was leading and sighed in resignation.

"OK I'll get my coat, you want to go now don't you?"

James nodded, together they got up and fetched their coats before leaving the house.

1864

George sat at the small writing desk in his bedroom and furiously scribbled his letter in the best handwriting he could muster, then continued, considering his situation. A week had gone by with little change to his circumstances and deep inside he knew his previous ploy had failed. He knew it was almost time for his stepparents to come in and see that he was 'all right' but he didn't trust them. He fought back a tear as he remembered what it used to be like before…

Before…

He stopped and closed his eyes to shut out the thoughts. He knew deep inside things could never be the same again, which was why his letter had to be finished in time.

As far as he could tell, there was only one person in the household that could be fully trusted, and he desperately hoped that Annie would be the one to bring his breakfast to him in the morning. The candle flickered then steadied again. He dipped the pen nib into the ink well, then continued writing. He'd begun to suspect the doctor was involved with his stepparents and whatever plan they had for him. It was something to do with the manor, but George in his innocence couldn't fathom what.

A muffled sound, much like a scraping of a foot on the wooden floors made him freeze and he quickly raised his makeshift shield up to the candle to hide its glow.

The scraping sound stopped and his heart and lungs seemed to do the same but then the scraping carried on down the hallway and he managed to breath a sigh of relief.

If Annie could slip his letter out to Uncle Arthur, then his torment might come to an end? He was sure his stepparents, or so called guardians, were up to no good and if he could just alert Uncle then things surely would improve. Telling the doctor his fears however, had been a bad move as he was sure that's why he'd had a good hiding from the old bag Mrs Cording the other night after he'd told the doctor he was being kept prisoner.

He finished the letter, quickly folded it up just like Annie had shown him and placed it underneath his pillowcase. Snuffing out the candle he climbed onto the bed and pulled the skimpy sheets over himself as he tried to fall asleep, praying that it would be Annie that would come in the morning.

#

Morning and the sun tried to push through a gap in the curtains casting thin rays across the dusty room.

There was a light tap on the door and then it opened as Annie came into the room with a tray. George didn't want to look in case it was his stepparents but Annie whispered his name and he let out a sigh of relief. He hugged her as she put the tray down with his meagre breakfast almost spilling out onto the floor.

"Now, now Master George, just be careful. If I spilled this you know they'd have me thrashed."

"Sorry, Annie. I've done the letter, here it is." He fished it out from under his pillow and she quickly pushed it into her bodice. She dare not put it in her pocket as that's where they'd look if her own suspicions were right. Annie had an inkling they were on to her as she'd been silly enough to ask about the scars George had mysteriously developed on his legs. They'd dismissed it as an accident and told her to mind her own business or be sacked. Somewhat blunt was that Mrs Cording and she shuddered as the thought of her passed through her mind.

Ever since George's parents had died and the Cordings had taken over she'd seen his health slowly deteriorate. She was now convinced that his only living relative, Lord Silverwright, didn't know that the persons he'd entrusted to look after his nephew were treating George badly. But to what end, she dare not think. All she knew was that George had initially trusted Dr Frederickson, the physician to the manor, with his worries but it would seem to appear the so called 'good' doctor was in league with the Cordings.

George had turned to her for help when she quietly told him she had seen the scars and wondered how he'd got them. Reluctant at first, George had burst into tears and told her how he'd been beaten for being a liar and telling the doctor so many lies about his stepparents. She knew she had to get the letter to Lord Silverwright but making sure she could get it out of the manor was going to be a different matter.

"Annie, I'm scared, I keep feeling that I'm being watched. It's happening now and he's over there beyond the wall yet I'm sure he's there." She looked sympathetically at him and shook her head.

"Now then master George, I'm sure it's nothing and you are getting yourself all worked up now so that you are seeing things. There's nothing but a solid wall there."

She patted George on his head gently and helped him get dressed for the day even though he was no longer allowed outside to play. The sunshine was so inviting that morning, but the servants had got strict instructions that George had to be kept indoors as he was 'unwell'. Annie knew differently but dare not challenge the doctors advice to the current caretakers of the manor. She would have to bide her time and choose the right moment to post the letter.

#

The present

They walked up the path towards the main graveyard in the direction of the church, noting there were several other people visiting graves, changing flowers or removing dead ones that had seen better days from vases.

James instinctively headed over to his family's gravestones and stood silently in front of them for a few moments. Sally stood just behind him giving him time to pay his respects but all the while casting a glance around to see if she could see the Victorian gentleman, but to no avail.

It was almost twenty to three now and she spotted the Reverend Cossant coming down the path. As she was close she recognised Sally and came over to her.

"Hello, you're Mike Freshman's companion, aren't you?" Sally looked at the reverend speechless for a second or so, then regained her composure.

"No, Mike was my mentor and for a time my boss and, yes a close friend but we were never, you know, that close. James is my partner and it was Mike that got us together before he died." Sarah Cossant looked mortified at her mistake.

"Please forgive me, my mistake, although I knew Mike for a few years. He always had glowing praise for you and dare I say a little twinkle in his eye whenever he mentioned you. I'm sure James would understand, especially if it was Mike that brought you two together in the first place."

Sally smiled and nodded realising the reverend had clearly forgotten that Sally and James had been together at Mike's funeral, then had a thought.

"Have you seen that Victorian looking chap I mentioned a few weeks back? James and I wanted to ask him a favour, but we only ever seem to see him here."

Sarah looked puzzled.

"I've never seen the person at all, I remember you asking about him and I've also asked a few regulars if they've met him but I'm afraid he seems to be a bit of a mystery. Perhaps you've seen a ghost?" With that she chuckled a little then gave her excuses and carried on her way.

Sally felt a bit annoyed as it seemed the reverend wasn't paying any serious attention to the matter, but then on reflection why should she? She looked round, spied James and headed over in his direction.

Meanwhile James stepped back from the gravestones and immediately felt a chill come over him. He turned and just a little further up the path, sat on the bench, was the gentleman he and Sally sought. He noted Sally was quite far down the path and was talking to the reverend so plucking up courage he walked over and stood in front of the gentleman.

"OK it's time we had a chat you and me, the game is up and I want to know what is going on and who put you up to this charade."

The gentleman got up and turned to James, a look of surprise mixed with a hint of satisfaction upon his face.

"I'm not quite sure what sort of game is up dear sir, but perhaps I ought to now inform you that I can play no game with you, for I'm..."

James felt frustrated with this and interrupted him.

"I don't care. I'm not interested I tell you. Just tell me the truth and get to the point."

"That really is a great shame sir, as I had put great store by your help and young Jennifer did imply that you were the one to ask. I see now that she was wrong in her perception of you. I'm sorry to have troubled you"

The gentleman turned to leave but now James had snapped to attention.

"What do you mean? Jennifer? You mean my sister? I don't understand – how come she appeared to you? Only I can see her!"

The gentleman turned back to face him again and smiled knowingly. "And therein lies the problem. You see I didn't want to say it out straight away for you might not have believed me but allow me to demonstrate." He stepped closer to James …

#

Moments later Sally came down the path and immediately noticed James sat on the bench with the strange gentleman from the previous week next to him.

"Oh, good to see we've met up again. How long have you been here and what's your name?"

James was strangely silent and she thought at first he hadn't heard her even though she was a mere couple of feet away from them both. However, James just looked up at her then swung his arm at the gentleman. She was about to shout at him to stop when her throat dried up and she could barely speak.

James' arm swept through the upper half of the gentleman's body and he in turn smiled and doffed his hat to her. She sprang back in shock uttering a few choice profanities and James got up and rushed over to her, holding her by the waist as she settled down after the shock of realising she had just seen a ghost.

White faced now and breathing heavily she edged to the bench and sat down where James had been sitting.

Nervously, she shuffled away from the gentleman whilst staring at him intensely as James stood there and took a deep breath.

"Sally, meet Arthur Silverwright or more properly, Lord Arthur Silverwright."

He paused, then added… "deceased."

7: Lord Arthur Silverwright

Sally blinked several times in quick succession at the word 'deceased' then tentatively reached out her hand but quickly withdrew it as it passed through Sir Arthur's arm. She trembled slightly and remained silent, somewhat shocked, not knowing what to say or think. Lord Silverwright smiled and did a slight bow to her.

"I must apologise my dear. I never wanted to startle you and hoped to ease you into knowing my state but alas it was not to be." He looked up at James then saw a young couple in the distance heading along the path towards them. "May I suggest you sit down next to your dear lady? Those two will not be able to see me and I fear it may look rather odd if you are speaking to an empty space."

James nodded and sat down between Lord Arthur and Sally who remained motionless and was clearly somewhat distressed by what had just transpired.

The couple walked past them and politely said 'hello' to James and Sally, James reciprocated whilst Sally just nodded blankly at them. As they walked away, Sally and James could have sworn the girl turned to her partner and whispered that Sally looked like she'd seen a ghost. They seemed to laugh at something and carried on up to the church entrance and stepped inside.

"You're not real…" Sally muttered as she looked past James at Lord Arthur.

She was still in a daze and her scientifically trained mind was jumping through various hoops trying to get a grip on what she was experiencing or possibly hallucinating; yes, that was it, she thought to herself. She mentally repeated it to herself, she was hallucinating that's all.

The hallucination spoke to her.

"Not in your physical sense, no I suppose I am not. May I ask you both if you would kindly go across the graveyard to the other more secluded path and take up residence on the bench you will find there. It is a little more private and less chance of you looking rather foolish talking to thin air."

James turned to Sally and shrugged but Sally was open mouthed trying to say something to him. She gave up and just turned round to find Arthur had vanished.

"SHIT! He's just, just, gone! Right in front of me he just… disappeared!" James held her hand and they both sat there trying to take in what they were experiencing. He looked into her eyes.

"Welcome to my world – fun, isn't it!"

James took in a deep breath and was about to say something else when a young girl's voice seemed to whisper in his ear. "Go to him James, trust him, he needs you like I did." James turned quickly to look for the person and realised he was looking straight towards his family's grave. Jenny stood there and nodded at him before fading away as Sally turned to see what he was looking at. James stood up and motioned to her to follow but she hesitated, staying seated.

"James, is this real? Are we unwell or something?

People don't come back from the dead really, do they?" She stood up next to him and took his hand. He tried to smile at her and again put his arm round her waist and held her close to him.

"Again, welcome to my world. When it was last year and I was seeing Jenny, I thought I was going mad. Yet somehow I held on and with your help I discovered I had a lost sister and even managed to see my long dead father whom I'd never met. So, no, we're not going mad. We're privileged to be able to see Lord Arthur, what's-'is-name. Jenny was just standing there by her grave and I heard her tell me to help Lord Arthur so I'm going over there to see what he has to say. Are you with me, love?" He looked pleadingly into her eyes and she looked back into his.

"Yes. No matter what I've been led to believe, it really is a case of seeing is believing even if I can't explain it. Best not mention it though to any of my colleagues in the force – they'll be carting me off to the funny farm if they got to know any of this!" They turned and looked across the churchyard but couldn't see any other sign of a path so together they walked back up to the church entrance.

Passing round the crumbling yet still quite ornate stonework, they spied Lord Arthur sitting down at another bench just like he'd said and they walked over to him along a path they hadn't noticed before. To be fair they had not needed to come to this side of the church so that there was no wonder they hadn't known about it.

Before they could sit down however, Lord Arthur stood up and pointed to an engraved plate affixed to the bench.

James bent down and read out loud.

"To the memory of a dear Sister and Brother-in-law who tragically died within months of each other in the year of our Lord, 1864." Before he could read any more, Lord Arthur sat down and they joined him, although Sally nervously kept to the end of the bench, keeping James between herself and Lord Arthur.

"My Sister, Charlotte and her husband, Nathaniel Ferrymore, died within months of each other and are laid to rest over in the corner. They were the Lord and Lady of Grasceby Manor at the time. You can see their graves from here although sadly it seems this part of the graveyard is much neglected. This is why I had this bench dedicated to them, so I could come up and sit here paying my respects. That was when I was alive, but it never came to pass I'm afraid.

I was always under the impression they were quite healthy. Charlotte died first, apparently of consumption when she was away visiting our only living relative, Aunt Ethel a dear friend of Alfred Tennyson. You may have heard of him?" James and Sally both nodded in unison and he continued.

"Nathaniel was naturally grief stricken but as they had a very young son, George, my nephew, Nathaniel soldiered on. Four months later he had a business trip in Paris to attend to, but died at Grantham before he could reach Dover.

His horse is supposed to have bolted and reared up throwing him against a wall and crushing him before anyone could help.

Very odd as he was an experienced horseman and knew his horse well. Most peculiar indeed.

However, around two months after Nathaniel died, young master George also died, apparently of pneumonia. I thought it was simply a tragedy as the diagnosis was by a very trusted family friend, Dr Frederickson. But my suspicions were aroused when, let's just say a friend in the household whom I held very dear, apparently was fired, left the manor and I was not able to trace her whereabouts afterwards, she appeared to have simply vanished."

James looked at Sally who sat looking incredulously at Lord Arthur and he knew she was wrestling inside with herself, trying to reconcile that she was seeing and hearing a ghost. Lord Arthur was about to continue when the church clock began to chime for 3pm and he looked up at the church tower and clock, then quickly back to them.

"I will have to go, my time is almost up for now. Please come here again won't you as I ne…" The clock bell struck 3pm and Lord Arthur simply faded from view causing Sally to stand up and back away from the bench. James went to her, concerned, but knew she was close to her limit of strange things happening, he braced himself as he saw the look on her face.

#

1864

"Ahh, Annie, I was wondering where you were."

Annie, shuddered at being discovered just as she was trying to sneak out to catch the postboy on the quiet.

She had not counted on Lady Cording, as Mrs Cording informed everyone to now call her, being up so early and to be standing at the side entrance.

"I wanted to get an early start M'lady and thought I'd heard the postboy. He's a bit early today though if it is him. I did right did I M'lady?"

"Hmm, yes I suppose you did. Let me know if there is anything from Lord Silverwright." Lady Cording turned to go but had noticed Annie was nervous and there was a suggestion that something was amiss, especially when she had mentioned Silverwright's name. She turned back to Annie noting that something was in her petticoat pocket. "Whatever it is you have in your pocket, you will hand over to me THIS INSTANT!"

Annie shuddered. This was her worst nightmare as she had not placed the letter inside her bodice not expecting to be stopped so early in the morning. She had no choice but to comply. She handed over George's letter and feared the worst. Lady Cording tore the letter open and quickly read it. She looked harshly at Annie who squirmed at the scrutiny. "Have you read this?" Lady Cording demanded and Annie lied.

"No M'lady, I was asked to post it, was I wrong to do so?" Lady Cording was surprised and disappointed by the reply and shook her head.

"No, no, you were just doing your job. Thank you, Annie. However, you will not discuss this with anyone, understood? That will be all."

Annie curtsied and quickly left, sick to her heart that she'd failed George. Lady Cording watched her go and snarled at her.

She knew Annie was lying and she would pay for it if it was the last thing her ladyship did.

She took the letter into the study and placed it into the front cover of the book she knew her husband was currently reading, knowing he would come down in an hour after having his breakfast. She knew that if a letter like that reached Lord Silverwright then their plans would unravel and they would face ruin and possibly prison. She hurried out of the study, she had other things to attend to and needed to see the doctor, best her husband not know all of what she got up to or had organised. He was aware she had feelings for Dr Frederickson but turned a blind eye considering what they had planned.

Annie watched her leave as she peered from the barely open kitchen door. She thought about entering the study to retrieve the letter but knew that if it went missing she would be the first person they'd come to for questioning. However, she did slip quickly into the study and picked up a couple of sheets of paper and a sheet to fold over it for the cover. Fortunately, she knew Lord Silverwright's address, she'd occasionally received a letter from him for herself, letters she treasured greatly.

Annie knew that if she quickly wrote a brief letter to him about George's plight, he would come up to investigate for himself. Taking the papers with her to her room she sat down and hurriedly wrote as much as she could whilst desperately praying that the postboy had not already arrived and departed.

Finished, she addressed it and hurried downstairs again only to meet 'Cook' walking from the side entrance towards the 'post table' with a delivery of letters in her hand.

Annie's heart sank and this time, instead of putting the letter into her petticoat pocket, she stuffed it inside her upper inner garments. Just in time as Mr Cording, or Lord Cording, as he also liked to be called now, walked downstairs ready to partake of breakfast in the dining room.

"Come along wench, get my breakfast and be quick with it as well!", he boomed, and headed for the post table, He picked up the pile of letters walked into the study dropping them on the writing desk and headed back out to the dining room. Annie did as she was told and hurried into the kitchen. She knew though that George was in for a rough day when Mrs Cording returned.

She also knew if she tried to warn him, then they'd both be in serious trouble but if she could just hold out until the next mornings post and send her own letter, at least they'd have a chance to get one of the letters off to Lord Silverwright. The one saving grace was that the manor had an account with the local postmaster so she wouldn't need to pay for the postage.

She should have taken her letter back up to her room.

Late afternoon and Annie would swear on the holy bible that she could hear George crying in pain as the Cordings punished him for writing the letter to his uncle.

She was allowed to take George his evening meal to his room where he was confined; her heart broke as she looked into his tear stained face, he threw himself into her arms and sobbed until he could sob no more.

Annie struggled herself and inside she determined to make sure her own letter would get posted and that somehow Lord Silverwright would get to know about how his nephew was being treated.

Hurrying out of George's room, she headed downstairs but, as she approached the door to the study to go past and into the kitchen, the door was flung open and Dr Frederickson called to her.

"Miss Annie, a word please, in here." He gestured to her to enter the study.

She did as she was told. She knew she couldn't disobey him.

'Lord' Cording and her 'ladyship' stood in front of the writing desk looking stern, whilst the doctor took Annie by the arm and squeezed it tightly. Mrs Cording walked up to her then slapped her across the face, causing a trickle of blood to flow down from her nose. Annie stood frozen and shocked at the turn of events.

"So wench, I know you lied to me this morning about the letter. It was too well written for it to be just that little brat on his own. We know you try to protect him and that you have 'feelings' for his Uncle. How disgusting that is for a mere low life servant such as you! You should know your place – in the gutter!"

Mrs Cording looked carefully at Annie's uniform then grabbed at her top and pushed her hand inside roughly, causing Annie to flinch. She pulled her hand out with Annie's own letter held tightly and Annie's heart fell like a stone. She knew she would get beaten for this outrage. Mrs Cording ripped open the letter and quickly read it, scowled, then tossed it to her husband. She stood in front of Annie menacingly. Mr Cording read the letter then passed it to the doctor who scanned through it and nodded, grimly.

"You know this can't go unpunished my dear girl? Regardless of your supposed connection with Lord Silverwright, he can't protect you here can he?"

Annie was shaking now and shook her head, her voice gone with fear at what they might do to her, "If you come quietly with us now then no harm will come to George. Utter a single scream or word and it will not just be you who will be punished severely tonight. Do you agree?"

Annie nodded positively as much as she could whilst trembling at what lay ahead. Mr Cording grabbed her by the arm and forcibly made her follow him and his companions out, across the hallway to a door and down the steps into the basement.

8: Annie's fate

Mr Cording held her tightly by the left wrist, causing Annie to flinch with the pain; he guided her across the cellar floor to an odd-looking contraption. It appeared to be an iron framework, box-like structure with two rings on one of the upper bars and two rings on the lower section close to the floor.

"A little contraption I came up with for punishing those who disobey, or simply upset me or the wife." Mr Cording said as he made her bend over the box and he tied her wrists tightly to the upper set of rings causing her to whimper with pain. Annie knew she had to endure what was to come for the sake of George but it didn't make it any easier to bear the pain of the thrashing she now expected to take place.

Mrs Cording walked round to the front and bent down to sneer in Annie's face. "So you think you are good enough for a lord do you? Think you are better than us? You are nothing but filth, girl, only fit for the gutter, I can tell you. Thought you could sneak those letters out did you? This is what you get for the trouble." She nodded at Mr Cording as the doctor stood off to one side but he called to both of them to listen to him.

Annie could not see them for they were behind her, but an animated discussion was certainly taking place in hushed tones and then it went deadly quiet. She heard footsteps come up behind her and suddenly a rag was whipped round over her face and stuffed into her mouth; tied tightly behind her head so she could not speak.

The pain was almost unbearable, she tried to scream, but couldn't.

"It's for your own good my dear." The doctor said as he stepped back and leaned against a couple of barrels. She was shaking with fear now and knew that at any time she was going to wet herself but had to keep some composure. Mr Cording stepped up behind her and, along with his wife, they grabbed her legs at the ankles and spread them as wide as they could to tie them firmly to the lower contraption rings. Annie tried to scream again but the rag was too tight. This was wrong, she expected to be whipped but why tie her by the ankles?

Mrs Cording then took great pleasure in firmly gripping Annie's upper garments with both hands and then tearing them at the seams. Ripping her upper layer off she then grabbed the undergarments and tore at them until Annie was naked from the waist up. She continued to try to scream but the rag was too tight. She guessed this was the time they'd whip her now and she steeled herself ready.

She was wrong.

Mr Cording then stepped up to her and grabbed her lower dress and tore at it, then at her undergarments until they too were torn away and dumped on the floor, leaving poor Annie completely naked. Shaking and terrified, her three antagonists stepped back in disgust as she wet herself in sheer terror and began to sob uncontrollably.

Mrs Cording grabbed one of the torn garments and roughly wiped Annie's rear until it was dry but sore from the rough handling.

She stepped back and nodded at her husband who proceeded to drop his trousers and underwear and prepare himself.

The doctor looked on completely detached without a care in the world as Mr Cording advanced, then forced himself on Annie, causing her to recoil in shock at this violation. Mrs Cording looked on, knowing she was glad it was the wench and not her, as she knew her husband could be very rough. Unlike the doctor, she remembered and stole a glance in his direction. Finally Mr Cording was spent and stepped away from Annie. Annie tried to find something to mentally hold on to and she kept thinking that it was protecting George.

"You were right my dear. A real joy!" sneered Mr Cording. Dr Frederickson turned and winked at Mrs Cording whilst Mr Cording wasn't looking and he too now undid his lower clothes and took his turn with Annie as Mrs Cording averted her eyes from the sight of the partially naked doctor. Annie could no longer resist and tried to whimper as the tears rolled down her pale red and puffed up face.

Finished, the doctor stepped away and tidied himself up but Annie's ordeal wasn't over yet. Mrs Cording walked across to one wall and took a whip from its resting hook. She walked up to Annie from behind so that she couldn't see what her 'ladyship' was about to do.

"Now, wench, this is from me!" The whip was raised and suddenly brought down ferociously onto Annie's back causing blood to ooze from the strike. Again and again as Annie tried to scream, five, ten, twelve, the lashes kept coming.

At fifteen, Annie finally slumped unconscious against the bars. Mrs Cording stopped and a sickening smile of satisfaction took hold of her face.

Dr Frederickson walked over to his medicine bag and opened it up to rummage inside. He fished out a small glass bottle and a rag and carefully took the stopper out of the top of the bottle. Holding the rag over the open end he upended the bottle and back again so that a small amount of the liquid was taken up by the rag. Putting the stopper back in place, careful not to sniff the aroma, he walked over to Annie.

"A quite recent innovation and possibly a revolution in medicine if used the correct way. A shame that she won't actually know she's died." He said as he put the rag over Annie's nose. There was little reaction as she was already unconscious, but the doctor knew it would give them more time to finish the task he had decided on.

Mr Cording walked to the back of the cellar and after tipping out its contents, brought a large sack over to Annie motioning to the doctor to help him. Untying her from the apparatus they bound her wrists and ankles, bundled her unconscious form into the sack and tied it tightly.

"Our gardener, Mr Godfrey, dug over the vegetable garden at the back this morning, so it's nicely disturbed, and easy to dig deep. A good place to get rid of her I think." said Mrs Cording.

The two men nodded and between them began to carry the sack up the stairs whilst Mrs Cording hurried up ahead to make sure no one was about.

Annie's fate was sealed…

9: Repercussions

"James…" Sally hesitated, "We have to talk."

They'd driven to his home after the encounter with Lord Silverwright and Sally had not uttered a word until now as they stepped through his front doorway. James took his coat off and offered to help her with her own, but Sally shrugged him off. He knew deep down this was not going to go well.

"No, I'm sorry James but, but this is too much for me. I'm a Detective Super in the police force and I'm used to dealing with all manner of things, but… but ghosts are something else. Give me a normal crime, anything, and I'm at home doing my job but the supernatural? That's, that's…"

She shrugged at her loss for words and looked down at her shoes. James took her by the hand, led her into the front room and sat her on the sofa.

"Sally, don't you think I'm feeling the same? I'm a computer programmer, software engineer… to many a geek when I was young. But I always worked with things I understood and could explain. I never asked to start seeing ghosts, it just happened and it took me months to come to terms with that. I still struggle now, heck I have no idea how they occur or why I don't see every single dead person that's ever walked the earth. So, I just accept that there is something going on that I have no control over and it's one of those things that hopefully one day science will come up with an answer for."

She looked at him but shook her head and got up.

"I need time James, time to let all this sink in. We've got a lot on at work what with cutbacks and yet still having to deal with idiots, vandals and the like. At the moment I just can't have this going on in my life as well. It's beginning to affect my work and I can't have that happening."

She took his hands in hers and stepped up to him, kissing him lightly on the lips then backed away towards the door.

"I need a bit of space and time to deal with this. Don't think ill of me love, I do indeed love you but I need some breathing space. I'm sorry, I really am." She opened the door, hesitated and looked into his eyes then stepped out closing the door quickly behind her. James opened it though and stepped out onto the front pathway.

"Sally!", he called out.

She stopped and looked back at him but was clearly close to tears. James hesitated, then sighed, knowing her mind was made up.

"Don't leave it too long. I'll be here for you when you're ready." She nodded and walked over to her car with her back to him so he couldn't see her crying.

#

His lordship paced up and down in his study whilst Jack stood patiently waiting for Lord Grasceby to settle down.

"I'm at my wits end Mr Hammond, I can tell you. I have the landscape gardeners coming to start on the lake tomorrow and the interior work is way behind schedule.

It's no good I tell you, no good at all!"

Jack looked at his lordship and indeed felt a little sympathy with his plight. He knew that the manor needed a lot of upkeep, that this was the last stab at trying to make it a modern enterprise to stave off bankruptcy.

"Your lordship, I do sympathise with you, but my men are adamant that they've seen things that shouldn't be in any decent world of ours."

He paused and took breath. "I think however I may have a part answer to our prayers though. I made enquires of my own. I didn't find out much from the innkeeper but as it happens, I discovered by accident that your own estate manager, Charles, may know something that can help."

Jack nodded over to the doorway where his carpenter John stood. John opened the door to his lordship's study and beckoned to someone to come in. Charles stepped through and politely nodded to his lordship.

Jack turned to Charles. "Go on Charles, tell his lordship what you told me." Charles looked squarely at his lordship but was clearly a little nervous.

"Well sir, if you remember we had that funny business with 'Wolds View' cottage and that missing lass case. From what I heard on the grapevine, it wasn't just the two detectives who solved it but a chap called James Hansone as well.

Apparently, if Mrs Lieter at the Post Office is to be believed, his wife had been asking if anyone had seen a ghost of a girl at the cottage and hinted that her husband had seen her on several occasions.

Rumour had it that he'd seen her close to where her body was eventually found. What with being friends with detective Freshman, this chap Hansone unofficially helped the police to convict Richard Dreyer. I suppose he might be able to help but he does keep quiet about it and seems to shun any publicity."

Lord Grasceby looked thoughtful for a few moments then looked at Charles. "Yes, nasty, unpleasant business that Dreyer had kept hidden all these years. Who would have thought it of such an upstanding member of the town. Wasn't this Hansone the chappie that found the old original De Grasceby Manor ruins? Yes, I remember now, that's why we ended up giving the archaeological society permission to undertake a dig on my land in a few months' time. Hmm, I think he owes me a favour. Have you got his address?"

Charles nodded, fished a piece of paper out of his pocket and handed it over. Lord Grasceby waved at Charles to leave, who was only too happy to get back to his own work and not worry about such daft nonsense about ghosts at the manor. Although he shuddered as he remembered his own ghostly encounter in the woods near to the discovered ruins, but quickly put it out of his mind.

Jack looked at his lordship and realised he was lost deep in thought, so he bade his farewell and left, motioning to John to follow him.

Perhaps now, he thought, they might be able to hold onto the contract for the renovations. It was a big enough contract for him to have passed over several other requests for work so the last thing he needed was for it to all unravel, ghosts or no ghosts!

Secrets of Grasceby Manor

1864

He awoke from a bad dream. Annie was standing over him and urging him to run but she kept turning into Mrs Cording snarling at him and that's when he woke up. The room was dark and he shivered even though he didn't feel cold. It was like, what did his parents used to say? Someone walking over his grave.

It had been a dismal day only broken by watching the gardener from his window digging over the vegetable garden. Later that afternoon had been awful when he'd suffered a beating from Mrs Cording. He'd forgiven Annie when she came to see if he was alright after the evil Mrs Cording had found his letter. Annie comforted him as much as she could and promised that she'd already written another letter which she showed him. She was going to try again in the morning.

His thoughts came back to what had awoken him. He got out of bed, wandered over to the window and peeped out of the curtains to look out at the garden. Weak moonlight filtered through patchy clouds on the other side of the manor gently illuminating the garden and he could roughly work out where he was looking.

Movement off to the right caught his attention.

There were three or four figures, he couldn't quite be sure, moving along the garden path with something slung between two of them. He stood back alarmed then crept back and carefully made sure there was barely a crack in the curtain line from which he could continue to watch.

His breathing grew heavy as he began to realise the shape they were carrying could be a person and he watched with increasing terror as he recognised Mrs Cording leading them along the garden path. They stopped and it was clear there were four people as one of them handed shovels to two of the party and they began to dig.

Very deep! Very deep indeed…

It seemed like an eternity before they stopped, then unceremoniously the person sized sack was swung into the hole. What looked like garments were also thrown in and under the moonlight, George gasped as he recognised, they were like the ones worn by the servants.

"Annie..?" He barely whispered to himself as he watched the party shovel soil back into the hole and he backed away unable to watch any more. His thoughts reeled as he tried to dismiss the terrible notion that the Cordings had indeed killed Annie and were burying her even as he thought this.

If they could do that then what about… He rushed over to the bed and buried himself under the sheets trembling and scared out of his little mind as he began to cry uncontrollably.

Mrs Cording looked back towards the manor and caught movement from one of the windows. She realised it was George's bedroom as his curtains seemed to sway even though the window was closed.

"I'd swear that the little brat has seen us, been watching from his window." She said to Mr Cording, Dr Frederickson and Godfrey the trusted gardener they'd brought to the manor when their plans began to work.

"Godfrey, finish this off whilst we go check on the boy." Godfrey nodded and the three others headed to the back door of the manor.

Godfrey was no stranger to criminal activities and owed the Cordings a lot for their help over the years, so he picked up the shovel again and continued to fill the hole covering its sinister sack with soil. He'd make sure only he dug in that spot if needed from now on.

Once inside the manor, Dr Frederickson pulled the Cordings to one side.

"Listen, we have to be careful here. We can't be certain he was indeed looking so Mrs Cording, you quietly go see if he is asleep. If it's clear he's spotted us then we will have to do something about him but it's better for our plan if we can deal with him much later.

We have to come up with an excuse about Annie's disappearance as well, as the other servants will be wondering where she is and may start asking questions."

Mrs Cording was about to complain but her husband held her hand and shook his head. He beckoned for her to go upstairs so she reluctantly did as she was told.

Little did he know she was silently cursing her weak husband as she headed quietly up the stairs.

Carefully opening the door to George's room, she heard barely a sound, faint breathing coming from the bed. She closed the door and made her way downstairs again.

George trembled in his bed as his mind replayed what he'd seen and he fell into a troubled sleep.

10: Drawn to the Manor

James was not really in the mood to talk to the person standing at his front door, but when his lordship stated who he was and why he was there it at least took his mind off Sally and he allowed Lord Grasceby to enter the house.

"I apologise for the intrusion Mr Hansone, but I really am at my wits end and I am hoping you might be able to help out. I'm willing to pay for your services as well, so please don't think you'd be out of pocket."

James gestured for him to sit on the lounge chair whilst James sat down on the sofa across from his lordship and shook his head.

"I always thought Charles would spill the beans one day. Guess it serves me right for snooping around the cottage last year. OK, so for now I'll hear what you have to say then I'm afraid I'll have to ask you to leave. I'm no ghost hunter your lordship and it is beginning to cost me dear so I'm not really happy about this."

Lord Grasceby smiled but was a little perplexed as he was not aware that anyone else had approached Mr Hansone prior to this day.

"Well that's as may be, I am led to believe you have had some, shall we say, 'paranormal experiences'?"

James nodded slowly but didn't offer any comment.

His Lordship continued. "Well, apart from the fact that I gather you were trespassing at 'Wolds View' cottage last year.

You may be aware from the recent news coverage that during the renovations at Grasceby Manor, some of the workmen have seen things. Odd things, mainly a young boy and recently a servant girl as well. It has caused friction between myself and the firm responsible for the renovations. Something which I quite frankly cannot have at this stage, renovations that if not completed in time, may well lead to my financial downfall.

Old stately homes such as Grasceby Manor require a great deal of expenditure on them in this modern world of ours and I can tell you that the income from the estate no longer keeps up with that expenditure. These are difficult times I can tell you.

That is why my wife and I decided to take the chance on renovating the manor and opening up to the public to bring in more revenue. I'm sure you can appreciate that today tourism is even more popular and with the current interest in history I think we have a chance to turn our fortunes around.

But not if the workers continue to be spooked by whatever it is they keep seeing. I have looked back through a few family documents to see if I can find anything but alas, there doesn't seem to be anything to explain recent sightings. Family history doesn't seem to have been a family trait as my ancestors don't appear to have kept much in the way of records, apart from a few portrait paintings down the ages.

However, in the meantime I would really like for you to come over to the manor and simply have a wander round to see if you see anything unusual."

James looked about to say 'no' and in anticipation his lordship played his trump card.

"Of course there is the little matter of you trespassing at 'Wolds View', I'm sure if you can take a moment to help out then I can find it in me not to take that matter any further."

James listened to all this and seemed to be aloof but his mind was already going over the meeting with Lord Silverwright. There was also his own sighting of the boy a few days earlier when he'd stopped outside the manor walls. He knew that inexorably he was being drawn into whatever had happened and indeed was currently happening, at Grasceby Manor.

Deep inside he knew he couldn't escape.

"OK Lord Grasceby, I've listened to you and I certainly feel for your plight. Let me think about it and I'll get back to you if I feel I may be able to help. As I said, I'm no ghost hunter and never asked to see anything like that but I'll sleep on it and get back to you. Fair?"

His lordship smiled and stood up.

"Indeed sir, I am indebted to you for at least listening to me. I do hope you do decide to help and I certainly look forward to hearing from you again if you can see it in your heart to help. You know where to find me."

James followed him into the hallway and saw his lordship out. His curiosity was peaked however, so he went over to the sideboard and opening a drawer, took out several folders with the papers he'd printed out from the files he'd found at the archives and began to go through them.

#

Secrets of Grasceby Manor

1864

George woke up, sweating, he shook his head hoping and praying that he'd only been dreaming again. He realised that there had been a faint knocking on his door and for a moment he was puzzled. Annie had a firmer knock, Annie...

The door opened slightly and Heather peeked round to see if George was awake. Seeing him looking at her she quickly came in bringing with her a meagre breakfast tray and placed it on his bed.

"Oh master George, they want us all downstairs shortly in the study for an announcement and I can't find Annie. Has she been in, to see you this morning?"

George trembled, not knowing whether to tell her his fears but all he could do was shake his head. Heather looked deeply troubled.

"Quickly now, let's get yerself dressed and we'd best not be late or I'm sure there'll be trouble. Annie is sure to be sacked if she doesn't show her face in time. Heaven knows what's got into her to be away like this."

George quickly did as he was told and dressed. He took one look at the so called breakfast and he turned away from it. Heather muttered something about wasting it but the feeling down in the pit of his stomach wasn't going to contend with the slop the Cordings now sent up to him for 'breakfast'. Heather took the tray, paused as George stood up and made sure his clothes were tidy, then they headed downstairs, firstly into the kitchen to get rid of the breakfast tray, then round into the study.

Heather led George by the hand as he tried to steal glances looking at the servants and people gathered but he couldn't see any sign of Annie and he felt himself begin to tremble. On seeing Heather take George over to stand next to Dr Frederickson, Lord Cording stepped forward with a stern look on his face.

"I have gathered you all here this morning and you may well note there is one person absent. I have summarily dismissed the wretch Annie from her work here and she is not allowed to ever return. Last night before Lady Cording retired upstairs to bed, she heard a commotion come from this very room and naturally she investigated. She discovered Annie rifling through my private letters. In amongst them she had discovered my key to the safe and was attempting to unlock it. It was a despicable betrayal of everything the previous lord and lady had believed of her and it is unforgivable."

The servants began muttering amongst themselves unable to believe the news and Lord Cording had to slap the writing desk hard to get them to quieten down.

"She has not just betrayed us but you and indeed little George here by her devious actions, I had no choice but to sack her once Lady Cording called for me to attend. She left late last night and if any of you even think to talk to her if you see her in town, then you too will be dismissed. I will not tolerate this sort of behaviour in this house. Do you understand me?"

They all muttered again but it sounded as if they were accepting his word without question for fear of losing their jobs.

George realised he was trembling and felt short of breath.

Heather spotted his discomfort. She stepped forward and did a small curtsey in front of Lady Cording.

"Excuse me Ma'am but I think George is having some form of fit. May I take him to his room and look after him until he's recovered?" Lady Cording looked at George and her eyes seemed on fire but she just nodded and waved Heather to take George away with her. Heather scuttled out of the study with a dazed George in tow as Lord Cording turned to the remaining servants assembled.

"And another thing. From now on the only person allowed into the rear garden, other than her ladyship, myself and the doctor, is Mr Godfrey. It is not a playground for idle hands or souls and he will be cutting down the wretched maze at the side, to make more space for growing our own produce and give us more room for the pigs to fatten for later in the year. Mrs Bottomly, ensure Heather is also informed of this once she returns from looking after young master George. You are all dismissed. Get back to your duties."

They all scurried off, all except Mrs Bottomly.

"Begging your pardon your lordship but I've brought up Annie since she were a wee nipper and this is not her. Perhaps she was possessed by something, a demon perhaps? They say it happens a lot or so my cousin Meg has told me, she..."

Lord Cording's vicious stare stopped her in her tracks.

"People can change Cook, I personally would not have believed it myself if her ladyship had not caught her red handed.

No more talk of this and get back to the kitchen. I'm sure there is plenty to keep you busy and not engaged in idle gossip." She curtsied and left but she knew deep inside, things were not right. Annie would not have done such a thing, at least not without reason, but she also knew that his so called 'Lordship' would not hesitate to dismiss her and so she bustled her way back to the kitchen to begin preparations for later in the day.

Dr Frederickson walked over to stand in front of their lordships.

"I sadly do think George may well suspect at least part of the truth. You will need to keep an eye on him but I feel we will have to bring forward our plans regarding the little brat, the longer we leave it the more chance that he will convince others to get a message to his uncle before we are ready."

He reached into his bag perched on the writing desk and fetched out a small container. "This is a tincture I have prepared similar to the tincture I used on the wretch, Annie. In small doses it will render him unconscious if added to his final drink of the day. What I suggest is that when he is unconscious, open his bedroom windows wide so the room gets quite chilled and leave him exposed to the night airs. After around a couple of hours, close the windows and put him back in bed.

Repeat this for several nights and with luck he will catch a fever and so will appear to die of natural causes.

I am meeting his uncle in London in four days time to finalise the details of George's will and will be ensuring that you two will become the sole beneficiaries of the estate if and when George dies.

I implore you not to do anything stupid with regards punishing the boy in the meantime while I am away otherwise it could ruin everything. Am I clear?"

Lord and Lady Cording nodded although there was a hint of resentment in Lord Cording's eyes at being told what to do. Nonetheless Dr Frederickson left later that afternoon for London and the Cording's knew that with luck it was only a matter of time before Grasceby Manor was theirs.

11: A fleeting glimpse

Lord Grasceby himself opened the door and James stepped through. "I'm so glad you've come along, I was getting quite nervous that it had been a waste of time. Is there anything you want whilst I'm here?" James looked about and took in the rather posh décor and surroundings. He could see why it would cost a fortune to look after the manor. His lordship coughed politely to get his attention.

"Sorry your lordship, very impressive indeed. OK, may I simply wander round the manor to see if anything happens? As I told you I'm not really a ghost hunter and I don't know how this works or even if it will just be a waste of time for both of us."

"Oh quite, indeed, feel free to look over the whole place but naturally regarding our bedrooms on the upper floor I'd prefer if possible to leave them alone. The sightings have been seen here in the hallway, over there in the kitchen and upstairs on the first floor hallway so I expect those are your first places of inquiry. Incidentally if you need me I'll be in the study to the left of the kitchen." James nodded and looked towards the kitchen.

"Very well then, I'll start in the kitchen and take it from there." Lord Grasceby started towards the study then stopped.

"Oh, by the way my daughter's wretched cat, Mr Shabernackles – no don't ask, appears lost. Heather, that's my daughter, hasn't seen him for at least a day and she does get frightfully upset when he disappears like this.

Normally he comes back within a day or two but if you happen to see him, somewhat fat fluffy thing he is, then let me or indeed Heather know."

James smiled as he remembered the cat and Heather from the other week and then he proceeded into the kitchen.

It looked like a mixture of a blast from the past with large pots and pans hanging along one wall, to a fridge and separate deep freezer at the far end. The sink next to a wide and spacious window looked as if it was hardly ever used yet the old fashioned kettle had seen better days. The air seemed cool but he noticed the back door was open and inquisitively James stepped through into the back garden.

You would never know from the front road that such a large garden existed at the rear of the property. Former stables lay off to the right and the seven foot high wall extended all around the property. The gate to the yard between the stables and the manor was propped open and James spotted a JCB digger a third of the way down the garden parked up and silent.

"Guess that's one way to deal with such a large garden" he chuckled to himself. But jumped out of his skin when a little voice piped up behind him.

"That's not for the garden silly, that's for our big pond daddy is having made." Heather stood looking up at him as if he was stupid. She'd wandered into the kitchen looking for Mr Shabernackles, saw James through the kitchen window and recognised him from the other week.

James regained his composure and looked down at her.

"Hello Heather, seems like we are destined to meet again after all. Have you found Mr shasberwhatsits yet?

"It's Mr Shabernackles. No and I'm very cross with him. He likes to disappear, ever since the men came in to do some work for daddy. I think they spook him and they should be told off. Well, all except the young boy, he can come and go as he wishes."

James attention picked up.

"So, you've seen him again then, this boy, what's he like? Can you describe him to me?"

"No need to, he's over there." She pointed towards the yard and James spun round… only to see young Simon and his older colleague Phil who were examining the stonework of the stables. James grimaced and turned back to Heather.

"No, not them, the other young boy…" He noticed Heather keenly watching Simon but kept James just between herself and the two workers. "Soo, you like Simon then?" Heather went all coy, then stood her ground.

"Huh? No, don't really like boys, just cats. Mr Shabernackles is much more fun." She peered from behind James again then seemed to have a change of mind and did a small wave at James and walked back into the kitchen and out of sight. He looked back towards the workers, smiled to himself and then headed back indoors into the kitchen then out into the hallway. Heather was certainly a character he mused as he looked about then decided to walk up the stairs to the second floor.

Thirty minutes later, pacing up and down the hallway on the second floor, he had nothing to show for it.

James' heart knew that he seemed to be on a fools errand and wasting his time. He entered what originally had been a bedroom in the past apparently but was now used for storage and gazed from its window out across the stables and yard. He could just see the road on his right with the brick wall enclosure almost hiding it and he figured the two end rooms of the Manor either side faced north and south.

He'd seen the boy looking out towards the north and standing in the eastern window of that room so he made his way back out into the central hallway and across to the doorway. It was locked and he grimaced.

"Huh, so much for having access to all the rooms on this floor." A meow came from behind and as he turned there was the cat, Mr Shabernackles, sat looking expectantly at him. "What do you want then? You know your owner is looking for you and she's worried?" He asked but the cat just looked up at him and began doing what all cats seem to like to do, lick its hind quarters by being an extortionist.

James turned back to the door forgetting for the moment that he'd already tried it and gave the handle a twist.

It opened. "Oh!"

He stood there somewhat bemused and turned back to Mr Shabernackles who continued to lick himself and pay no attention.

James stepped through into the room and had to work his way past what seemed like hundreds of boxes before he could reach the left hand window where he'd seen the boy. It was a good view and he could now see the road where he'd stopped and then been joined by Heather just a few days earlier.

He turned back, almost falling over Mr Shabernackles in the process and he briefly cursed the cat who sat and stared back at him with an innocent air about itself. James shook his head and continued to inspect the room which stretched for what seemed like half the length of the building. A few hunting pictures, somewhat faded and in poor condition, adorned the back walls but it was clear the room was no longer in regular use. A box held a portrait of a family in it but otherwise there seemed nothing of interest for him.

"Well at least I'm being paid regardless if I find anything." He muttered to himself and wandered back into the hallway followed promptly by Mr Shabernackles. Lord Grasceby came rushing up the stairs and surprised both James and the cat.

"So sorry dear fellow but I forgot something." His Lordship walked to the end room James had just left. "I'd forgotten I had locked this room as we keep many of our older possessions in here that are not in use." He promptly unlocked the door as James stood and stared, lost for words. Mr Shabernackles sat and just looked at him. His Lordship nodded and promptly headed back downstairs noting the cat and mentally thinking to himself he should let Heather know.

James walked back to the now unlocked door, opened it, looked back inside then closed it as he came back onto the landing hallway.

"Well I'll be..."

Mr Shabernackles seemed intent on tripping James up as he walked down the hallway to the end room which faced southwards across the rear garden.

The hallway landing itself turned left and ran along for several metres before turning back on itself forming a U shape in the centre of the manor. This gave access to all the rooms and James headed for the door on the right-hand side of the back and tried the handle.

This door opened instantly and he walked in but turned instinctively, looking back and down at the cat. Mr Shabernackles looked up and down at him and stepped towards the open doorway then stopped. He looked up at James but sat down keeping his gaze on what lay beyond the open door. Puzzled, James looked into the room and realised it was a library.

"Well, are you coming in or what then cat?"

Mr Shabernackles just stared at him expectantly but didn't move except to do a quiet meow. "Well stay there then." James stated to the cat somewhat indignantly.

He walked in and started to weave his way between several rows of bookcases towards the south facing windows. The room was much larger than the north front room and he suspected it was several knocked into one to provide more room for the library.

Wide arches maintained the structural integrity explaining the design. There were four windows looking out over the back garden and he looked out from the second from right window.

It was clear that Lord Grasceby's plans for the gardens were extensive and there was a marked out heart shaped area which James suspected had to be the planned pond, he noted that his Lordship was being a little over exaggerating by calling the proposed pond a lake.

The JCB was in view and now there were two workmen stood next to it pouring over plans. No doubt, he thought, they'd have their work cut out. One of them looked vaguely familiar but James couldn't think where he'd seen him.

He didn't notice Mr Shabernackles had entered the open doorway but the cat stopped stock still suddenly staring off to the far left at the little boy looking out the far window just as the boy faded from view. James turned to explore the room more, not noticing the cat and missing the boy by a split second as he carried on checking the views from the windows making his way around the long room.

Satisfied there was nothing going to happen he shooed Mr Shabernackles out of the door and back into the hallway and continued along and round the hallway entering the rooms one by one. Mr Shabernackles seemed to get bored and wandered back to the rear of the hallway and sat whilst James disappeared again into another room.

It looked up as a young servant girl seemed to come out from the closed door to the library and head downstairs fading from view when she reached the bottom.

Mr Shabernackles looked round as the other room door opened again and James emerged back into the hallway missing the spectre by mere seconds.

If only cats could talk…

#

1864

George's tear stained eyes tugged at her heart strings and Heather was not sure of what to do or believe. Once in his room he blurted out what he had seen the previous night and then told Heather about the letters he and Annie had written and how Mrs Cording had caught Annie about to post his letter. George implored Heather to write to his uncle but she felt torn.

On one hand if Annie had indeed been killed as George suggested then she too could end up with the same fate. On the other hand the story about Annie they'd been told earlier had seemed farfetched.

She'd known Annie for two years now, ever since Heather had been accepted in as a domestic servant to the original Lord and Lady Grasceby and kind-hearted Annie had taken her under her wing.

Annie wasn't a thief that was for sure. Heather wasn't as educated as Annie had been but she knew enough to know that she needed to play along and bide her time.

She reassured George that she would secretly try to help but he needed to keep quiet about her knowing the Cordings and Dr Frederickson were up to no good.

He nodded.

"Look out for Annie – I miss her and I know she's not a bad person." He implored and Heather's heart sank a little, wondering if indeed Annie was no longer with the living. She stayed with George most of the morning and after fetching him a light lunch she excused herself and went in search of Mrs Cording.

She had come to a decision.

"Yes, what do you want? I thought we'd told you to stay with master George?"

Lady Cording stood with her hands on her hips in the study glaring at her and Heather briefly wondered if she were doing the right thing.

"Sorry milady but Master George keeps telling me the most awful lie. He believes Annie was killed … by you and Lord Cording along with the good Doctor. I suspected he was a fibber when I first met him and never did like Annie, always seemed to think she was above the rest of the servants. I thought you should know." Heather curtsied and knew she was taking a gamble. Lady Cording looked at her then smiled.

"Good Heather, thank you for telling me. I am most gratified that you felt you should inform me of the lies that little weasel is concocting. Leave it to me and," she paused for a moment, "if you hear any more such ramblings then do let me know."

Heather curtsied again and left the study to go to the top floor and her cramped room but her heart was heavy knowing that George would probably suffer. However, she fortified herself with the thought that if she made the Cordings believe she was on their side she might be able to get a message out to Lord Silverwright.

One thing kept haunting her, where was Annie? She shuddered as the story George had told her played across her mind. It would explain why they were no longer allowed into the back garden, but Heather did not want to think about that for now. She picked up a leaf of paper and hoped she had enough ink for the task she'd set herself.

12: Preparing the way

It was a job. That's what it was, Joe thought to himself and operated the levers, expertly swinging the JCB around. Yet another bucket full of soil scooped from the ground where his lordship's pond was to be sited. He had to smile to himself at the thought that his lordship kept referring to it as his 'lake'.

"Lake, my arse!", he said to himself and chuckled. He emptied the bucket into the awaiting dumper truck then swung the digger around and began to scoop another bucketful.

Joe didn't mind and really enjoyed his work, especially as the contract to dig out the basic area for Lord Grasceby's large pond had come to the firm he worked for. It made a change from just digging out drainage ditches for the environment agency as he had been doing the previous year. Some year that had turned out to be, he mused and smiled briefly to himself.

Even more pleasing was the prospect of getting the work done ahead of schedule. That would get them a bonus, maybe it would pay for that long overdue holiday he'd promised his partner Steve several months back. Joe chuckled to himself as he remembered that drunken night on New Year's Eve when he'd made the resolution to treat them both to a holiday now that they'd committed to each other.

He looked at his watch; it was lunch time, so he lowered the bucket carefully into its safe position and turned off the motor.

The engine would have been deafening by itself but health and safety meant they all had to wear ear defenders now and he was glad to get them off. They made his ears all sweaty and they often itched like hell. He instinctively scratched behind his left ear, it was always the left one and shook his head. He wondered what Steve was doing now and as he swivelled in his seat, he picked up his smart phone and sent a quick text to him asking that very question.

Stepping out of the cab and climbing down, he walked over to the work's minivan and spotted his boss, Phillip, sitting in the driver's seat mulling over the plans.

"Lunchtime Mr Coates, if that's OK with you?" His boss was deep in thought then suddenly realised someone had spoken to him.

"Oh, blimey, that the time already? Yes, of course Joe. You got the usual then?"

Joe nodded and shrugged.

"I luv him to bits but for some reason he does want me to be on this weird diet the same as him. Tofu and yuk, it would seem. Have you got the usual?" Joe looked hopefully at his boss who grinned and nodded.

"Yeah, here it is, corned beef sarnies with mustard, just as you like them." Joe looked lovingly at the sandwiches and for a moment couldn't help thinking that he might be in love with his boss, if the latter weren't as straight as they come! Phillip was one of those rare things, a boss who understood what is needed to keep his workers happy in their jobs.

Joe sighed and tucked in to the sarnies as Phillip poured them both a cup of coffee each. Joe picked up his flask and feeling somewhat guilty, he poured the strange concoction Steve had made him, out onto the ground and then sipped from the plastic cup Phillip offered him. Despite being piping hot it slipped down the throat a treat and he guiltily enjoyed the caffeine boost. Better that than the peppermint tea that had only a short time ago been resident in the flask.

He looked over at the area where the digger was standing and surveyed it.

It was a simple job really, as all they had to do was dig the main heart-shaped hole down to a depth of five metres at the centre and a metre deep close to the edges. The landscape gardeners would come in and do the rest, but this would save a lot of backache for them. He knew his boss had been concerned at all the fuss over the so-called ghost sightings by the restoration builders working inside the manor. Joe thought back to just the last year, they'd had no end of trouble when Joe had accidentally uncovered the remains of a young girl missing for about fifty years.

The media, police and indeed the lord of the manor here had all been dragged in and for several months they'd had to suspend work until all investigations had been concluded. The environment agency had wanted the drainage ditches dug out and widened and had not been happy but neither he or his boss and friend, Phillip could have prevented it.

Phillip finished his lunch before Joe and looked about; towards the pond they were excavating, at the manor and towards the stables.

"So Joe, you seen anything odd then?" He asked and Joe shook his head. "Nah, and I don't want to either. Bloody business, there's no such thing as ghosts. Mind you Steve is the exact opposite to me and keeps asking when I get home if I've seen anything. Any of those shows on TV about it and he's glued to the screen with a cushion ready to put in front of his eyes if something spooky is shown. He is a daft 'un indeed but..." Joe sighed and rolled his eyes and Phillip chuckled.

"Chalk and cheese you two, that's what. Well let's get on then. I said to his lordship that we could do this inside a week."

Joe looked at him, bewildered.

"But it'll only take one more day, what're you going to do – we'll be done with a couple of days spare?" Phillip looked a little mischievously at Joe. "Does no harm to stretch the work out a little. Just don't go too mad that's all. Nice little contract for us but if we finish too early then he'll be suspicious. We'll get that bonus his lordship promised if we come in a day early so let's just make sure we do just that, eh?"

Phillip winked at Joe who just smiled back and appreciated how wily his boss was. In a way Hammonds men seeing the ghosts causing a delay had encouraged his lordship to offer Phillip a rather generous bonus if he and Joe would get their particular work done without any delays. So at least some good had come out of it, not that they were to let on to Hammonds and his men, heaven forbid mused Joe.

1864

George sat on his bed rocking slowly back and forth, clutching his hands around his knees; at a loss as to what to do. He didn't feel that well at all but knew he couldn't afford to fall ill if his fears were correct about Annie's fate. His fevered mind raced with wild thoughts as he thought back over the last few months and began to wonder if his parent's deaths had been planned. But what could he do? He was only seven and now his only possible chance at contacting his uncle appeared gone and he began to realise that even Heather was at risk if the Cordings found out he'd confided in her.

He heard a noise outside his door. He dropped off the bed and creeping over to it, he opened the door up carefully. Peering around there was no one to be seen and just a faint sound of pots being clattered down in the kitchen.

There it was again.

This time the noise seemed to come from inside his bedroom and he popped his head carefully round the door and glanced around the room but could see no one. Silly, he thought to himself, how could anyone have got in, they would have had to pass him. Then he noticed his toy room's door was slightly open and he wandered into his room and over to it…

A strange looking man stood inside.

"What are you doing in my toy cupboard?", asked George, puzzled and a little alarmed. The stranger looked at him, looked away, then faded from view as George stepped back in shock and started breathing heavily with fear.

He struggled to find his voice whilst fear tried to strangle him but finally, he shouted, a few moments later Mrs Cording rushed into the room to see George standing next to the toy cupboard, shaking like a leaf.

She smacked him hard after hearing his story of a strange man in the toy cupboard and went to leave, briefly noting the door to it was indeed slightly ajar, she closed it before leaving George to cry alone on his bed.

Evening came.

George's eyelids drooped ever lower until finally he slid into a deep sleep. Mrs Cording shook her head, she'd been waiting ages for him to drop to sleep. Each night for the last five nights, George appeared to be getting used to the concoction not realising what he was really drinking.

Mrs Cording had succeeded in convincing Mrs Bottomly and Heather that she'd had a change of heart and was now personally caring for George since he was so distressed at Annie 'leaving them'. Over the last few nights she had been frustrated as the weather had been quite mild but tonight there was a chill in the air and she thought she'd detected a roughness to George's breathing.

Soon, she thought, soon he will become seriously ill and they can let nature take the blame.

Lord Cording had received word from Dr Frederickson that the paperwork had been signed and indeed that stupid uncle of George's, Silverwright didn't suspect a thing, Grasceby Manor would become theirs in just a matter of weeks.

No doubt they would have to feign sorrow at the passing of one so young but they'd 'done their best' for the little mite.

They would have to concoct a story about Annie in case Silverwright started to question why she wasn't at the funeral. They were going to ensure the servants were not present so he couldn't speak to them but even if he came back to the manor, which was likely, the servants would be forbidden to mention Annie even if asked.

George was sound asleep now, she carefully pulled back the bedclothes and undid his night gown. She'd insisted that George wear a particular one she'd had made up, ensuring that it could easily be undone from the front. As he lay there naked, she walked over to the window and carefully opened it up. It slid a little noisily, she knew she'd forgotten to rub some candle wax on it but she slid it high enough to use a peg to wedge it in place.

The cool breeze wafted over her face and she smiled as she stepped back, then a strange feeling came over her as if she were being watched. She looked quickly round the room and noticed the toy room door was once again slightly ajar. She headed over and closed it, locking it so that George would not be tempted to play if he did awaken in the night. Still, she was a little puzzled about the door. She turned, shook her head and quietly left the room.

The cold night air began to seep into George's body and deep in his sleep he gave a little cough then settled down again not realising what was happening to him.

Roughly two hours later, at least by the time her candle had half melted, Mrs Cording returned, closed the window, redressed George and pulled the bedclothes back over him as he wrestled with demons in his sleep.

Morning.

Heather stooped over George as he'd woken shivering and after feeling his forehead, she rushed out of the room to fetch Mrs Cording. On hearing Heather, Mrs Cording had to suppress a smile and instead appear concerned as she hurried upstairs to George's room and felt his head.

He was sweating and looked very pale. George looked up at her. "Where's mother?", he asked. Mrs Cording turned to look at Heather. "Poor mite is becoming delirious." She turned to George. "She's dead, some months ago. Can't you remember dear?"

Before George could answer or even understand, she callously continued. "So is your father, thrown from his horse. You're in my care now." George was clearly struggling to understand her.

"But…but where's Annie, she always looks after me." He managed to say amongst fits of coughing. Heather was standing near to the door and Mrs Cording couldn't see her face as she struggled to stop herself crying.

"She's gone. She stole from us and was dismissed so no more talking about her, you understand me?" George looked at her with a glimmer of memory trying to assert itself.

"No, no it was you, you did something to her, you ..." He stopped, terrified at the evil, hateful look that had come over her face. Mrs Cording had hold of his arms and without Heather seeing she squeezed them hard so that he got the message and turned to look away.

"Heather, have Mr Cording arrange for the doctor to attend at his earliest convenience. Tell him George is frightfully unwell and I am very concerned about him."

Heather curtsied and quickly left the room. Mrs Cording grabbed George and turned him to face her.

"Now you listen to me you little wretch. There'll be no tittle tattle and wild lies you hear me? If I see you leave this room then you know what to expect, understand me?"

George just nodded, terrified. He knew his fate was sealed…

13: The extra room

Jack Hammond paced up and down on the gravel driveway as James stepped out into the sunshine. He'd seen Lord Grasceby and wondered if any of the workmen were around so he could ask them some questions. He hadn't realised that they were keeping away from him but it seemed that his lordship had phoned Jack; as he and his team were now standing on the driveway. Phil looked just as annoyed as his boss whilst Simon and John seemed to be taking it in their stride.

"I guess you're Mr Hansone then, the ghost chappie?", asked Jack and James winced at the description.

He shook Jack's hand.

"I don't consider myself a ghost hunter Mr Hammond and it would seem I owe you for me being dragged into this. I've had to arrange to take some of my spare holiday days to do this. All I want is to find out where each of you were when you saw something, is that too much to ask?"

Jack's face softened a little.

"Ok, fair's fair I guess. Phil…" He called over to the team by the van. "You saw things first – tell Mr Hansone what you saw on both occasions."

James was thoughtful as Phil walked up to him.

"Tell you what, let's go to where you saw things and take it from there." Phil nodded and led the way into the manor and through the hallway into the kitchen.

"I saw the lad here first and he seemed to be looking through me into the hallway.

When I turned to look, then looked back, he was gone. As I went out into the hallway I could have sworn I heard the name 'Annie' whispered, but I couldn't see anything odd."

Jack seemed a bit surprised at this last bit of information as Phil had not mentioned it to him or when he was accosted by the media a few weeks back.

James nodded and stood looking round the kitchen. "And?", he asked.

Phil hesitated.

"Well, a few days later I went down to the basement from yonder doorway to see what work it would need doing to bring it up to scratch. Big job I reckoned, and I wasn't sure if we'd be able to fit it in to the schedule as..."

Jack cut him off.

"Get to the point Phil will you!"

"Oh, sorry, well it was as I was about to walk back up the steps that the boy came down them and went straight through me. He carried on and disappeared next to the wall. That's when I rushed out and knocked her ladyship over. Caused quite a fuss and I left and went to the inn to calm me nerves, so to speak. That's when the reporter overheard me talking to Marcus and it all got blown out of proportion and hit the news."

James had forgotten about the basement and his lordship had also failed to mention it. He made a mental note to check it out.

"Wasn't there another ghost you saw down here in the hallway?" Phil was about to say something when Simon chipped in.

"I saw a woman. We'd come back to work and I was just coming in from outside when I saw Phil coming towards me, but I spotted this woman dressed like a servant glide down the stairs, turn and walk straight through Phil as if he wasn't there. Fair freaked me out it did!" Before Simon or Phil could continue, John pushed forward.

"Actually I gather that my sighting came just before that. I was upstairs on the second floor landing hallway and at first I just saw the cat, then Heather. She left and I turned round, only to have a boy matching Phil's original description standing there looking at me. Come to think of it he did look as if he was looking through me as well, as if I weren't there. He just turned and walked down the hallway and passed through the wall at the end. Jack just happened to come upstairs at that time, realised I must have seen something and asked me to keep quiet about it. He went back downstairs and not long after that he called me on my phone to say we were stopping work for that day. When I came downstairs, Phil and Simon were outside. They told me what they'd seen."

Phil joined in.

"What I saw was a black and white person-shaped blur walk through me from the stairs, sent me as cold as ice, then she went into the kitchen. Simon went to look but there was no one there and the back door was closed so whoever it was couldn't have got out that quick."

Jack was silent all the while this was going on but he stepped forward towards James.

"I didn't believe them at first and you can imagine I was initially furious at Phil for allowing the media to get hold of the story. But the looks on all their faces the second time round was enough for me. I don't believe in such stuff like ghosts but something spooked my lads. I can't afford not to finish this contract so what do you think?"

James looked round them and considered telling them about his view of the boy when he was parked up outside but something deep inside told him to stay quiet.

"Like I've said before, I'm not a ghost hunter and by the sounds of it the chap who was supposed to be one must have been a charlatan if he couldn't find anything. I do seem to think though, that the kitchen has figured a few times in this so perhaps that is a focus. I've been in there but haven't seen anything so far myself."

He paused, deep in thought for a moment.

"John, at which end of the hallway upstairs did you say the boy walked through the wall?" John scratched his chin and remembered he'd not shaved very well that morning as it felt rough with stubble.

"Far end, south side of the manor, it was as if he went into the library but not through the door." James nodded thoughtfully as he took this in and mentally noted to check out the second floor.

"Ok, thanks chaps. Sorry to have bothered you and got you to come in. I'll have a wander round and see if anything happens."

Everyone was about to go their separate ways when Lord Grasceby came down the stairs.

"Oh, Mr Hammonds, so you chaps are back at work then I see?" Jack looked at his colleagues and they shrugged as much to say 'why not?' so Jack nodded at his lordship.

"Good to hear we may be back on track then. How about you Mr Hansone, any progress?"

"No not really, but I'm going to have a look round upstairs, especially at the library as that may be a focus along with the kitchen." His lordship waved them all to continue and stepped out of the front door leaving them to it.

#

John stood next to James in the same spot where John had seen the boy. He felt the panelling on the walls and had a little chuckle to himself.

"Daft really as I couldn't reconcile the panels with the plans I was given. That's when I'd phoned Jack to come up and have a check of them with me; and before he came up Heather and her cat surprised me. Then the boy appeared just there…" He pointed close to where James was standing. "And he just walked away from me and through that third panel from the door on the right. I went over and into the library but couldn't see sight nor sound of him and haven't done since then."

They both walked down the hallway to the third panel and John tapped at it but just shrugged as it sounded no different to the others he'd been inspecting a few days back.

He turned to James.

"Tell you what, I'll fetch the plans from the van and you can tell me if I'm going bonkers or something!" He walked off and disappeared out of sight as he went down the stairs. James shivered and realised he'd left his fleece in the car. These old buildings he thought, always cold. He turned, then stepped back in shock.

The panel was no longer there and in its place was a door! Solid to the touch.

Was he having some kind of hallucination? He wondered. Regaining his composure slightly he reached forward, grasped the handle and turned it opening the door, fully expecting to enter the library.

And instead entered a bedroom.

James blinked several times and a creepy feeling came over him. Even when he'd first started seeing the ghost of Jenny the previous year, he hadn't experienced anything like this. He walked round the bed, it appeared to be well made but certainly not modern.

He looked around.

There was a writing desk, what seemed like a play area with several quite old fashioned wooden toys lying around and a small bookcase. The bed was close to the window and a small table was next to that with a candle stick, the wax half melted in its small bowl. On the bed were some clothes, a perfect size for a young boy. Again a chill ran down James' spine. Was he really here in the boy's bedroom and if so, why?

He walked across the room and realised it was smaller than the library so it seemed to be clear that at least two rooms had at some time been knocked into one to make space for the library.

He spotted a door at the far end of the room which would lead back into the hallway so James strode over and opened it...

...to find a toy cupboard crammed with toys of all shapes and sizes, most of them made of wood. He stepped into it as memories of his own childhood came rushing back. He turned, walked back into the bedroom, and looked back at the toy room and spied a rocking horse amongst the toys.

It shouldn't be like that. It should have opened into the hallway, he pondered. James walked back inside and stood looking for a second time at the toys in the tiny room marvelling at how good they looked. He realised that he was trespassing but was fascinated. He turned to leave only to find the young, but quite pale faced, boy in the doorway.

"What are you doing in my toy cupboard?"

James looked at him blankly for a moment, as he hadn't realised someone had entered the room after him. He turned to look at the rocking horse and turned back to explain...

...but there was no one there...

"Oh brother..." James went back into the bedroom but there was no sign of the boy and the room was unchanged. He headed back to the door and walked out and almost knocking John over.

"Where the hell did you come from?", John exclaimed in shock and James turned to point at the door...

...only to be pointing at the wooden panels instead. He looked at John who realised James was looking decidedly pale. "I think I need a stiff drink..."

Was all James could say.

1864

"But...but I did see him, I did, I did, I DID!" exclaimed a very weak George as Mrs Cording slowly lost her patience.

"Stupid boy, I've looked and there's no one there. You are trying my patience. The sooner you are gon..." She stopped herself, realising she'd nearly blurted out the truth. This sort of nonsense was probably only to be expected as he slowly deteriorated and perhaps he was beginning to become delirious.

"Good", she mused, "hopefully it won't be long now". She knew it had to look natural though, otherwise his uncle might suspect. Not that Arthur Silverwright had been that bothered about his nephew anyway. From what she'd heard from the servants, when George's parents had been alive, Silverwright had never really been that close to them and only saw his nephew a couple of times a year. Normally Christmas and when he was in the area, which was not often. Rumour had it however, that he'd apparently had a bit of a crush on Annie so they would have to be careful on that front.

The thoughts settled her as George slumped down in his bed but started a fit of coughing which didn't sound too good.

'Good', she thought and smiled inwardly with a deep sense of satisfaction at the boy's plight. Dr Frederickson was expected after six that evening and he'd be able to give them a better idea of how long the boy had to live.

Not long now.

Not long before the secondary plan could begin so she could be rid of that useless husband of hers ...

...and be with the true love of her life, Dr Frederickson

14: A shocking discovery

James sent yet another text to Sally but knew he was probably wasting his time as she had yet to reply to any of them. He sat on his sofa, switched the TV off and for a while checked out his social media pages, soon getting bored. It was getting late but he wasn't tired, so got up and fetched the folders of information he'd brought back from the archives the previous week. He had yet to search through them thoroughly.

He was still a bit unnerved by the ghost toy room. He'd always thought of ghosts as just people and perhaps animals, but rooms...? They were a different matter.

He started leafing through the printouts and managed after half an hour to get them sorted into some sort of chronological order. Unfortunately there wasn't a lot to go on, there was a very brief history of the manor with little of note. In fact it was remarkably boring! He already knew about the preceding 'De Grasceby Manor' and how parts of the unfinished manor had ended up being scavenged and used in both the construction of the village and later the modern manor. He had, after all, been the one to rediscover the ruins and inform the Lincoln Archaeological Society. And of course his lordship, Lord Grasceby.

He continued to browse through the notes in search of anything that could help.

The first Lord Grasceby to be based at the second manor, was from the Ferrymore family of Kingston upon Hull who were granted the lands by King George II.

From then on, what few references to the manor he came across always referred to Lord and Lady Grasceby rather than the surname of the family, so he assumed from that the manor had been passed down to family members since then. Interestingly there was reference to a change in ownership around 1866 to the Frederickson family. 'Ought to ask his lordship what his true family name is?', wondered James out loud to himself.

There was more information about the manor and estate after the Second World War but none of it seemed particularly relevant and nowhere were there records of any family details that seemed to mention a young boy or a servant girl passing away.

James leaned back on the sofa and sighed. Ironically his soon ex wife to be, Helen, was the genealogist and would know where to look. On thinking about her, he felt a surge of anger about her leaving him for his ex work colleague, Craig. That in turn brought Sally back into mind and he checked his text messages again in case he'd set it to silent.

No message from Sally.

James shook his head, pushed the papers back into their folder and headed up to bed in a bad mood.

#

The last couple of weeks had been tough as her workload had been very busy.

With fewer staff, Sally had been getting to her home very late almost every evening. She'd seen several texts come through from James and kept promising herself she would reply to him. She was missing him terribly and was beginning to feel foolish.

So, she'd seen a ghost, what of it? James had been right; he wasn't asking for any of it to happen to him or her. It must be as troubling to him as much as it was to her, so why had she been selfish and just left him to it?

Now she was investigating a spate of thefts near Short Ferry. Taking a few minutes off for a break, she had walked along the road and stood on the slender path on the bridge overlooking the Barlings Eau, a tributary that flowed into the nearby river Witham. She admired the sweeping vista and was in deep thought, James of course.

Suddenly the phone chirped in her hand as she was about to reply to his latest text. Startled, she dropped the phone … straight into the river with no chance of retrieval. She stood there with her hands on her hips in frustration.

"Bugger, that's all I sodding needed! I should have got that waterproof model." She peered over the railings but knew it was going to be hopeless to find it, there was silt, reeds and the current was flowing strong with a few hints of fish as they were swept along downstream.

Frustrated, she headed back to her car, drove into Lincoln to buy another phone and after phoning the station, planned to head home to reinstall all her apps and contacts. All this before lunchtime as well, she hoped the rest of the day would be better.

The road was busy; holiday traffic was already on the increase now they were into early May, so tourists numbers were on the rise. She reached Wragby and on an impulse slipped into the right hand lane instead of going straight on.

She had no idea why she had done that. The road would still take her to Bardney and then on to Horncastle, so she shrugged it off and thought of it being a pleasant diversion that might just put her in a better frame of mind.

She wound her way along the minor road then suddenly saw on a sign just ahead 'Grasceby'. She blinked at the oddness of her taking the route but took the turning nonetheless. Before she knew it she was driving along , round some bends, past the old airfield, RAF Grasceby, with trees either side and she knew she was going to be passing 'Wolds View' cottage any time.

Sure enough the trees seemed to drop away from the road on her left and there it stood, still empty but now with a 'sold' sticker across the 'for sale' sign. Sally sighed, she knew that James had talked occasionally about buying it but didn't think he had done, there had been no hint that he was being serious. Driving past, after around a mile of twisting minor road she entered the village of Grasceby.

She made her way round the village pond and as the road straightened a little she glanced at the wall surrounding the manor and wondered if James was there, but with a sigh she drove on by.

A slight bend and then she found herself slowing down as she neared the church and thoughts briefly turned to Lord Arthur Silverwright.

Her pulse quickened and she looked at her watch.

"This is nonsense, I've got things to do, not chase after ghosts!" She speeded up and drove past the church, out of the village and headed for Thimbleby and home.

#

"You know, really and truthfully Joe, you ought to say something to Steve." Phillip intoned as once again he passed over a pack of sandwiches that his wife had made for Joe. Joe looked down at his feet and grimaced.

"It's not easy though, he can be quite, well, sensitive and touchy if I comment on what he prefers me to eat." Joe looked at his boss shaking his head. "I know, I know, guess it has to be done but I just haven't found a way to do it yet without causing him any pain."

"Yes, but you both need to realise that you each have your own personal tastes and that is why you love each other – not for him or you to impose what you like on each other. The sooner you do it the better."

Phillip wanted to add that it was getting a bit much now as he and his wife seemed to be feeding Joe lunch every day when they were at work together. They ate lunch in silence for once and as they finished, they spotted through the gap between the stables and the manor, a car drawing into the driveway.

Phillip frowned.

"Looks like that ghost chappie is back. What a waste of time.

Hammond's men are stringing the job on so they can charge more if you ask me. They had that other ghost chap in and he found nowt, so I don't know what they expect. His lordship must be as gullible as they come." Joe just nodded but as he knew Hammond's man Phil, who'd apparently seen a young boy in the house, personally he kept his mouth shut.

#

James stepped out of the car and noted that Hammond's van was also parked up. 'At least they are working again' he thought as he entered the manor. Jack was in the hallway, busy looking at plans and acknowledged him as James passed by heading into the study.

There was no one there, his lordship was away for the day according to the calendar hung up on the far wall. A meow came from behind him and sure enough Mr Shabernackles entwined around his feet almost tripping him up, then sat, licking his right paw and looking up at him. James smiled at the cat and realised that Heather would be at school so he went to pick him up.

Only to regret it as he picked up the cat which suddenly hissed and pawed at him to be let go. James dropped Mr Shabernackles and cursed as he had a couple of scratches on his arm now.

He was about to curse the cat again when he realised Mr Shabernackles was not hissing at him but at the youngish looking servant girl just walking out from the study into the hallway.

"Shit!" He exclaimed and hurried out after her only to see her fade as she went up the stairs. He went up them leaving the cat in the doorway of the study. Mr Shabernackles was no longer hissing and had gone back to preening himself, unconcerned now with ghostly affairs.

At the top of the first landing, James caught his breath as he spotted the servant heading towards the library.

However, instead of going towards the actual door she appeared to open an invisible one then passed through the wooden panelling and James realised it was the same place he'd thought a door had existed a few days earlier.

He didn't have time to be spooked as he sprinted down the hallway and went through the modern door into the library but, on looking around, there was no sign of the girl. Bookcases, lots of them, filled the room including ones that extended up to the ceiling where they ran along the walls.

The library ran the whole length of this side of the manor and where there would have been at least two walls breaking it into three rooms, archways were in place to allow access to all the room yet still provide structural integrity to the building. He made his way round the bookcases and explored the whole room, but she was not there.

He turned then stopped suddenly as he spied through the second archway, not the Library, but instead the ghostly bed and bedroom he'd seen a few days before.

The view briefly shimmered and this time he did feel a chill ripple down his spine. He took a sharp intake of breath as he watched a young servant girl or woman appear to be tending the boy lying in the bed.

Suddenly they both looked his way and he froze expecting them to scream at him but instead the girl seemed to shake her head then pat the boy on his head. The scene faded and James felt light headed, holding on to a nearby bookcase for support. The library had returned to normal and the bedroom, boy and young servant girl were gone.

He took a deep breath and waited for his heart to slow down, then he left the room and headed back downstairs. John looked up at him and was about to carry on past to go back to his job and the panelling when he noticed the look on James' face.

"You OK Mr Hansone? Look a bit pale. Oh heck you've…"

"Yep, just had an odd experience I can tell you. I saw the servant girl go upstairs and when I went up into the library part of it seemed to shimmer and I could see a boy's bedroom with the boy lying down and her helping him. They're clearly linked somehow yet in my searches of the records there's nothing mentioned about them. Weird."

John looked a little sceptical but having seen the boy for himself he wasn't about to call Hansone a nutter.

Well not just yet.

He remembered that Hansone had suddenly appeared out of the panelling the other day and claimed there had been a door where there plainly wasn't one. It had spooked John somewhat.

James was deep in thought and turning headed into the kitchen, noting the back door was slightly open, just as he heard a muffled shout come from the garden at the rear.

#

Joe had his ear defenders on but had managed to fix his earpiece from his smart phone into the right hand side ear and was enjoying the heavy metal. Went well with the work he thought as he pushed the bucket into the ground and scooped up the soil.

He was now at the far end of the heart shape, working on the right hand lobe of the pond to be and he knew Phillip was pleased with progress.

Although rain had been forecast for later that day, with luck it would hold out until the evening when he would be at home cuddled up with Steve and hopefully a bottle of chardonnay. Ha, Chardonnay and heavy metal, who'd have thought it of him and he chuckled to himself.

The bucket emptied into the dumper, which was standing to one side of his digger, he swung it round again and dug in deep. Scooping up he lifted it and was about to turn towards the dumper when he noticed the fragile remains of some sort of large sack, parts of which hung from the buckets blades and he grimaced inwardly wondering what he'd found.

They were used to finding all sorts but last year had been the oddest when they'd found the remains of the missing girl, Jennifer-what's-her name. Still this was just scraps of material – perhaps rubbish buried long ago.

It was as he tilted the bucket and tipped the contents into the dumper that he spotted the skull as it dropped almost in slow motion from the upended bucket.

"Aww Shit! NOT AGAIN!" He exclaimed but the noise of the JCB drowned him out. He looked round to see if anyone else had spotted the skull and he realised there were several other white bones. Then he noticed Phillip standing off to one side with his mouth open in surprise. Phillip started waving and looked like he was shouting at him to stop so he pulled the earpiece out, moved the bucket to a safe point on the ground and turned off the motor.

Tearing off his ear defenders, Joe scrambled out of the cab and joined Phillip as they both peered into the dumper truck. The skull was partially buried by the other soil but there were a number of bones of different sizes lying scattered amongst the soil.

Phillip walked over to where the remains of the sack still protruded out of the soil and it was clear there were more bones and several items of clothing in a poor state.

Joe could hear his boss cursing quite loudly and knew this was not good for them. Thoughts of his bonus evaporated as he spotted James, quickly followed by another chap run out from the kitchen.

#

In the kitchen window Mr Shabernackles sat staring out at them watching intently, not moving a muscle as if he were a solid ornament. It was almost as if he were smiling…

15: The remains

Sally received the call late as she'd only just got all her contacts reinstalled on her new phone. The house phone had rung and the desk sergeant had explained he'd been trying to get her for twenty minutes on her old phone before realising she'd had to replace it. She jumped into the car and fifteen minutes later she arrived at the manor. She spotted James' familiar car, and for a few moments her pulse quickened but she wasn't there on a social call. A body had been discovered and, along with a forensic team that had also just arrived, she had work to do.

She walked through the manor guided by Lord Grasceby himself, whose worry was clear by the fact he kept wringing his hands.

"I'm on a schedule you know so I hope this won't hold things up for very long. I'm sure it must be an ancient burial thousands of years old and no need really for the police to be involved."

She stopped and looked at him squarely in his eyes.

"Your lordship. A body has been discovered on your property and whatever your schedule is, it is on hold until I say otherwise, do I make myself clear?"

He looked down at his shoes and nodded. Sally started walking across the grass towards the excavated area where a pond was apparently being dug out. Inside it and towards the far right was the digger with a dumper truck next to it and she could see her colleague, Harriet from forensics, bent over looking at something in the dumper.

She called out to her and Harriet waved her hand but carried on studying whatever it was that held her attention. Sally reached her but just then someone familiar stepped out from behind the dumper.

"James!" She knew she flushed upon seeing him and he smiled, uncertain as to how she'd react.

"Hello Sally. Err, I think you should talk to Mr Coates the foreman and Mr Galton. I suspect you have met them both before." She smiled, a little puzzled and nodded at him, walked round to the other side of the dumper to see the two men standing next to the digger.

"Well blow me, now that's a coincidence! You two found Jenny Portisham's body last year, didn't you?" Phillip walked up to her and spotted Lord Grasceby following behind her and the ghost hunter person, Mr Hansone. Phillip nodded forlornly.

"Yeah, and that set us back months as well. Looks like we're going to be stuck again with delays." He turned to his lordship. "I'm really sorry sir but looks like we can't finish until we get official clearance to continue working."

Lord Grasceby nodded solemnly and muttered something inaudible under his breath but didn't say anything else. Phillip Coates led Sally round to the other side of the dumper truck and pointed to a freshly disturbed patch of soil.

Sally walked over, looked at the remains of the sack protruding from the ground and could see several more bones sticking up inside. Crumpled up and very worse for wear was some other material that superficially looked a lot like clothes.

She crouched down and leaned over it to take a closer look just as James moved closer. He briefly admired the view then stopped himself and coughed a little to get her attention. She stood up and looked him in the eyes then leaned closer to speak into his right ear.

"Good to see you James. Listen, can't speak now naturally but don't call me…" James looked concerned at this and she hurriedly carried on. "No – I've got a new phone as I've lost the other in a river, and don't ask – I feel daft enough as it is. I'll text you alter when I've reinstalled my apps and contacts. As you are here, any connection with Silverwright and the ghost boy?"

James bit into his bottom lip.

"I'm not sure but we do have to talk as I've seen some pretty odd things here. Do you think it's the boy's skeleton?" She frowned shaking her head and wandered round to the dumper truck where Harriet had the skull in her gloved hands, studying it. She called out to the forensic scientist and got her attention.

"What do you make of it then Harry, and yes I know it's a skull but just humour me will you? How long since they died and could it be a young boy?" She glanced at James and mouthed to him 'how old?', James shrugged and mouthed silently six or seven years to her. She turned back to Harriet.

"Six, maybe seven years old or thereabouts." Harriet shook her head.

"Won't have an exact date for you until we can run lab tests, but looking at the soil type and sack remains I wouldn't think this is an ancient burial.

Sack material alone is more like the late seventeenth to mid nineteenth century by the looks of the weave. Plus the skull is not of a youngster, this is someone older, more like in their twenties. Always difficult to say but based on the hip bones, my suspicion is that this is, or I should say, was, a young girl or woman."

James tugged at Sally's sleeve. She turned and gave him a serious look as this was no time to be disturbing her whilst she was working. He leaned in and whispered into her ear.

"There's been sightings of a young servant girl and I've seen her a couple of times as well. She seemed to be connected with the boy." Sally pursed her lips deep in thought. She made her mind up.

"Harriet, you and Faraday," she looked around, "where is he by the way?"

"Oh he's just fetching some equipment from the van, he'll be here in a moment."

"Good, let me know what you think of the situation and possible cause of death if you can. See what you make of the rest of the sack, guess you'll have to be careful excavating it. I'm going to question the workmen for now." She turned to Lord Grasceby who'd wandered over to them after talking to Phillip and Joe. "Lord Grasceby, for now I'll have to cordon this part of the garden off so that forensics can do their job, I want no one other than my specialists here. Is that clear?"

He looked glumly at her.

"Guess I don't have much option. Can the other workmen continue in the manor itself?" She nodded assent and walked back over to James as his lordship headed back into the manor via the kitchen.

She leaned into James and pulled him closer so she would not be overheard.

"I, I.. I'd like to call round tonight if I can. Have a chat, you know, catch up and…talk about today?"

He smiled at her and nodded.

"Eight pm okay with you?", he asked. She frowned.

"Best make it nine as I'll have paperwork to do after I've talked to the two chaps who found the bones, with any luck Harry might have something for me too." He nodded and smiled dearly wanting to hug her but knew he couldn't whilst they were in public view. She smiled almost as if she knew what he was thinking, nodded, then went back to talk to Phillip and Joe.

Lord Grasceby looked at his watch as he heard another car draw up on the driveway at the other side of the manor and realised it was probably Lady Grasceby bringing Heather back from school.

"Oh fun, her ladyship is going to love this", he muttered and headed for the kitchen doorway. Meanwhile Mr Shabernackles silently watching everything from the kitchen window, continued staring towards the pond area.

#

It was almost nine thirty when Sally finally turned up at James' home that evening.

Eagerly he let her in and they passionately kissed and hugged for several minutes. Each kept apologising as they migrated from the hall into the main living room and collapsed onto the sofa.

"What a day, one minute dealing with a spate of thefts over at Short Ferry, frigging lose the phone as I take a few moments for myself, get a call out as a body has been found at Grasceby Manor and find you there – all on the day I was going to call you!" She snuggled in closer to him then noticed something. "Err, reckon I need a shower, mind if I…?"

"As long as there's room for two…" He chased her up the stairs and into the bathroom as she screamed with laughter and together they began to undress each other with eager anticipation…

They lay on the bed snuggled up in dressing gowns as James stroked Sally's right upper thigh. She shivered with the sensation and sighed. She'd missed this. So had James and he could only hope things were back to normal again. He'd had some hope as Sally had not retrieved any of the spare clothes she had started leaving at his place once they'd begun seeing each other on a regular basis.

He kissed her lightly on her forehead and she turned her face to look up at him.

"So…What's the story then with the manor, the servant and the boy?"

"Oh, am I under interrogation then Ma'am?", he teased her and pinched her thigh lightly. She in turn lightly slapped his arm then kissed him.

"Well, tell you what, I had an odd thing happen to me today"

"What, you mean other than everything you've told me so far?", he replied.

"You could say that, yes. I was heading home after getting the new phone in Lincoln and I had a sudden compulsion come over me to take the turning for Bardney at Wragby.

Next thing I knew, I was a few miles down the road and taking the minor lane that goes through Grasceby. I almost felt like I was being led to the manor or even, for that matter the church, but as I got close I felt foolish and carried on past and went home. If I'd acted on the impulse I would have been at the manor when they discovered the body. Spooky, don't you think?"

James screwed up his face.

"It's bad enough one of us is loopy, let alone the other." He chuckled and she politely elbowed him.

"Anyway, so what's this about a servant then?", she asked, so James sighed and proceeded to tell of all that had happened since their mini breakup.

When he'd finished, she looked thoughtful. "Well, now there is a police case concerning the manor I can take a look at our historical records and see if anything was reported. Any idea of the time frame?"

"You know if the two ghosts are linked then Lord Arthur did mention when his sister and brother in law passed on. What was the date…"

"Come to think of it, 1864 or thereabouts I reckon. Are you in work this week or on holiday?", she asked.

"Oh I had a few days owing to me so Mark let me have them this week. I'm back at work next Monday, so I've got a few more days still.

I'll go back into the archives in Lincoln tomorrow and see what else I can find. When will you know about the skeleton and what sex it is?"

She snuggled a little closer.

"Harriet is good, so with luck it won't be more than a day or so once she gets stuck in. She loves a mystery.

At least from our perspective it doesn't look like it's a modern crime, so it's not going to be high priority but I'll still see what I can come up with." He looked into her eyes and then looked past her at the alarm clock.

"Best get to sleep then young lady, otherwise you won't be getting up in time for work" Sally looked at him with a twinkle in her eye and slipped off the dressing gown.

"Sleep? No chance mister!" She winked at him as she pulled his dressing gown off.

#

1864

George came to his senses.

Despite the rasping cough, he knew he had to get out of his room and find somewhere to hide and he thought he knew where to go. Leaving the room, he was unsure of why the walls were oddly moving a little and as he walked through the building he knew it wouldn't be long before he was found.

The beatings and hidings he'd endured since his mother had died, didn't just cause pain and suffering, but confusion as well.

He just couldn't understand why his life had changed so quickly and violently. It was hard enough to lose his mother and father within a few months of each other, but to now be in fear for his life after witnessing what was probably Annie being buried…

The hallway landing seemed quiet as he crept along in his nightgown with a small candle as his only company, just about lighting the way.

During happier times he'd been allowed to explore Grasceby Manor as much as he wanted, as long as he didn't cause any mischief to the servants. On his explorations he'd found a small odd storage hole in the basement that, when he carefully asked about it, no one seemed to know about. Now he was heading gingerly down the stairs to it, to hide before his step parents could give him another beating, or worse, kill him.

Annie, his one true friend, had failed to get the panicked message he'd scribbled down, sent off to his uncle in, where was it, Chirester – Chichester? It looked like she had paid the ultimate sacrifice and he had a feeling that time was rapidly running out.

He stopped and suddenly held his breath as he heard something creak above him. He knew the layout pretty well and realised it was the main stairway and landing above.

He picked up his pace trying to shield the flickering candle flame, both to stop it going out and to hide some of the light spilling back giving away his position.

Again he heard a noise and suddenly in the distance he heard his name called out. He froze in terror as he tried to stifle a cough.

"George? George? GE-ORGE?" The voice was hushed but sinister. It was Mrs Cording and quickly changed from seeming concern, to an order. "Where are you BOY?"

George hurried on down the stairs until he was in the ground floor hallway reached the door he'd been looking for. Passing through, he hurried down the stone steps, almost tripping in his haste, but couldn't help giving out a little whimper as he seemed to be descending into the very dark depths of oblivion.

For a split second, he thought there was a person standing in the basement and his heart leapt but the figure faded as his candle flickered.

"George! Come back NOW and I won't be too harsh on you boy, not this time at any rate!"

The voice was joined by muffled sounds suggesting there was more than one person now searching for him.

George was now in the basement and his heart quickened, as he was close to where he'd discovered his little hideaway. The odd looking metal framework was new to him but he skirted round it as he noticed a dark ruddy stain on the floor. His heart skipped a beat in fear at what it might represent. He clutched the small package of food he'd snatched earlier from the kitchen and started across the floor towards his destination, when suddenly a lantern illuminated the room from above, just enough for him to be plainly visible.

"I'VE FOUND THE LITTLE RAT, HE'S IN THE BASEMENT".

The voice boomed and the lantern swung wildly as the person holding it raced down the steps and bounded across the floor, grabbing George roughly by the arm, pulling him down onto the floor. A rush of sounds above, descended down the stairs as George squealed in pain. His captor was joined by Mrs Cording and Dr Frederickson who towered over him as he lay on the dirty floor cowering in the flickering light.

Mr Cording raised his hand, about to thrash George, when the doctor stopped him.

"Now, now Henry, he's not really worth it and we need to do this properly, so hold your temper."

He turned to George. "So what did you think you could accomplish down here young master George, we were bound to find you so why try to hide?"

George cowered but tried to look up at the doctor.

"I thought I could trust you, you were my FRIEND!" He looked quickly between the doctor and Mrs Cording and thought about trying to run for it, but the doctor's hand reached out to him and he was momentarily confused. Dr Frederickson spoke more softly now.

"I am George, I am. Now take my hand, there's a good boy and we'll go upstairs and say no more about it." He turned to the other two "Shall we?" He looked at each of them and they realised what he meant. George hesitantly reached up, but the doctor suddenly snatched at his hand and with a firm grip hauled the boy up and into a body lock.

George started to scream but Mr Cording quickly put a rag into his mouth and tied it in place, whilst between them Mrs Cording and the doctor held George's legs and arms and bound them expertly so he couldn't escape.

Mrs Cording stared into George's terrified eyes.

"Lucky for us the servants are in their quarters on the top floor – don't want them nosing around and hearing you now do we? And one former wench will never wake up, will she master George?

We saw you watching us. Yes it was your beloved Annie! Huh, so called future master of the house. Not if we can help it."

She looked nastily into George's frightened eyes, smiling at him as he squirmed, and they started up the steps. The rag in his mouth came loose and slipped off and he bit angrily into Mrs Cording's arm. She jerked back, instinctively letting go of George's shoulders.

As if in slow motion, George's trussed up body twisted round out of Mr Cording's grip and he fell over the side of the steps, crashing onto the hard floor several feet below with a sickening thud as his head hit first.

He jerked violently, went into spasm several times before finally stopping; his life force spent. The Cordings and the doctor rushed down the steps but there was nothing they could do.

Dr Frederickson looked at the shocked faces of his two accomplices. "You idiots, you've killed him! It was supposed to be a natural looking death!"

He looked again at the lifeless form on the floor and thought for several minutes, holding his head in his hands, as the Cording's could only look on, exchanging worried glances between them. Finally the doctor came to a decision.

"Martha."

He hardly ever used her first name in front of Mr Cording lest he suspected there was something more to their 'friendship'. "We'd best get him cleaned up and put in his bed. Don't let any one in to see him. Just say that I think he may be contagious and only you and I can enter. I'll come visit him in the morning as if I'm checking up on him and you'll need to make a show of crying and running downstairs to tell the servants he has died in his sleep. I'll wrap him up and cover him on the pretence that he may still be contagious. That way no one will be any wiser."

"What if someone gets suspicious and he gets dug up – they'll see he didn't die naturally. They'll come for us I'm sure" panicked Mr Cording.

"Leave that to me. He won't be in his coffin. I have an idea about that. Now, let's see, he was coming down here to hide so what had he found that made him think he could elude us?"

The doctor started looking round and moving the smaller barrels and crates without any sign of a hiding place. Walking carefully around the edges of the room, he stood and turned, puzzled, then noticed something on one side where the floor seemed to be a slightly different shade of colour. He smiled at the other two and walked over to the spot.

"Change of plan" he said, as he bent over and examined what he'd discovered.

16: The gruesome details

Sally moved her phone away from her ear as, on the other end, Harriet terminated the call. She started the car up, indicated to leave the lay-by and headed back to HQ and the path-lab, wanting to see for herself. A quarter of an hour later Harriet let her into the room and beckoned her to come over to the display next to two tables, one with a skeleton on and the other with the neatly laid out but badly decomposed clothes.

"Well I've confirmed our skeleton is female and probably around twenty two to twenty five. There's no actual evidence of foul play in the form of violence, as none of the bones are broken. But get this, her hands and feet were tied and by the looks of it, there may have been a gag. In fact there are some rag fragments in amongst the soil samples and I've found incredibly tiny traces of an early form of chloroform. The sacking must have sealed enough to prevent it leaching through the soil into the groundwater.

This servant did not die naturally Sally, she was killed. I suspect quite brutally but in a way that hasn't survived the time in the ground. If her skin had survived intact we might have found more evidence but as it is, that's the best I can do." She stopped speaking then checked herself, suddenly remembering something.

"Oh, and the other material we found is definitely the sort of clothes that a servant from the early nineteenth century would have worn, but here's the other odd thing which I find worrying; she wasn't wearing any clothes at all.

These were just dumped in the same place but not in the sack. They were also torn with many of the buttons forced off, as if she literally had her clothes ripped from her."

Sally shuddered at the thought.

Harriet continued. "If you were to ask me and I know you would, then I suspect she may have been tortured, probably knocked out then...", she hesitated, "Buried alive. I guess one small consolation is that she probably never knew she died."

Harriet stopped and looked expectantly at Sally who was always amazed at her colleague.

"Bloody hell Harriet!", was all she could say. She turned to look at the skeleton laid out neatly on the table and the clothes laid out on the table beside it.

Harriet just smiled.

"We were sort of lucky in that she was buried quite deep but it seems the ground was never saturated. If it had have been, there would have been a greater degree of decomposition of the material of the clothes and probably of the sack as well. Still, this doesn't tell us who murdered her, just that it's clear she was indeed murdered and, as I've said, quite brutally."

Sally nodded but was deep in thought.

"Have you got photos of the servant's clothes and is it possible to reconstruct how they might have looked on the girl? For that matter, would you be able to simulate her facial features for me?"

Harriet looked puzzled.

"What good would that do you? You can't hold an identikit parade, anyone who was involved would be dead now!"

Sally smiled to herself, knowingly. "Oh, it's just curiosity and it would be interesting to compare her likeness with some of the family portraits that are on Grasceby Manor's staircase. You never know if she was actually some illegitimate child of one of the lords of the manor."

Harriet again looked puzzled.

"As this is no longer a high priority then why are you so interested? That's a lot of work and will take about twenty four to forty eight hours to complete and that's a lot of processor time for something that took place a couple of hundred years ago."

Sally looked straight at Harriet.

"Call it a burning desire to see justice done even though it was a long time ago." Sally smiled sweetly at Harriet, who just nodded, knowing when Sally had something up her sleeve. They walked out of the room together parting company as Sally headed up to reception to sign out.

#

"I wonder what her name was then...", mused James, as Sally recounted what Harriet had told her as she stepped through his open door and into his arms.

"You OK to be telling me this?", he asked worried that Sally might get into trouble. She held him by the waist and looked him squarely in the eyes.

"Look, somehow you and I have got dragged into this and as long as you don't mention what I've told you, then we're OK."

She let go of him and he sat down on his sofa.

"Yes officer, OK, I've trawled the archives but had no luck with any nineteenth century missing persons. Heck, I had better luck with Jenny than I've had with someone with no name, so there's no wonder I'm struggling. Grasceby Manor appears a boring place in history, as it seems nothing significant ever occurred there.

The interesting thing is that around the mid to late eighteen sixties, the manor changed hands from the Ferrymores to the Fredericksons which does seem to coincide with the date of both Ferrymore's deaths that Lord Arthur told us about. But he didn't mention a servant in all this. I've also found the birth and death certificates of a certain George, Hamilton Ferrymore, aged 7 who died of a fever in 1864 not too long after his parents – sounds like our ghost boy to me, so why did Lord Arthur imply the boy went missing?"

Sally sat down next to him and absentmindedly rubbed her chin, deep in thought.

"You know he didn't seem to get the chance to tell us more because he suddenly faded away. Come to think of it the first time, before I knew he was a ghost, he seemed suddenly agitated and had to leave as if he'd overstayed his time."

She looked at him then at her watch, but sighed. "It was always close to three o'clock in the afternoon, I wonder why that would be?

Perhaps it's time to go back but it'll have to be tomorrow after midday as I have a meeting to attend from 9am to 11:30am."

James smiled at her, a little in astonishment, considering her last reaction to meeting Lord Silverwright. She noted his expression and raised her eyebrows.

"Yeah, OK, I know, it's not what you expected but if you can cope with ghosts then I should buck my ideas up. Anyway I want to find out more about this servant girl. He may be able to tell us more and if we can do it before 3pm he'll probably be able to stick around long enough to tell us what he knows."

James nodded then noted the time.

"OK, shall we meet at the church at about 1pm then? In the meantime shall we go out for a meal, or stay in?"

"In, but how about ordering a pizza, that and a glass of wine and I'll be happy."

He nodded and reached for his phone.

#

1864

Lord Silverwright received the news of his nephew's demise and immediately set off for Lincolnshire. Ironically, he knew from his mother's comments, many years before, that tragedy dogged their family with several generations being wiped out, often in quick succession, but he had thought such things the ramblings of a superstitious mind.

Now he was not so sure.

First his dear sister Charlotte had perished, then a few months later his brother-in-law Nathaniel, whom he had held in high regard as an accomplished horseman. Now poor little George. He dearly wished he'd found more time to visit them all but instead he'd allowed his business ventures and explorations abroad to take up all his attention.

His only consolation would be to see the servant girl Annie, although he knew it would never amount to anything. He had enough on his plate and would not have the time to come up and manage the Ferrymore's estate at Grasceby. However, his schoolboy friend Dr Frederickson had convinced him that the Cordings were worthy to inherit and continue running the estate on his behalf.

He arrived and attended the funeral. He was pleased but saddened when he saw the seat dedicated to his sister and brother-in-law had been installed outside the church, reasonably close to their graves, as he had requested months earlier. Sadly he realised he would now need to have the plaque changed to reflect the loss of George.

He would see to that after his far eastern business trip was completed. Annie was absent and on enquiring, was informed that she had left with little warning after Lord Grasceby's death and her whereabouts were not known.

Indeed, the Cordings had searched high and low to tell her of the fate of poor George, but to no avail. He left Grasceby saddened that he had not seen Annie and immediately returned to London to prepare for a voyage to Singapore on business.

Arthur would never get there. Six months later on-board ship, after a stopover at Bombay, he contracted malaria and whilst in a feverish state he began to hallucinate. George appeared to him pleading for help several times and insisted that Annie and he had been murdered. Lord Silverwright struggled with the nightmares until finally at 2pm British time, he succumbed to the fever and the next day was buried at sea.

It would take another eight months before news would reach Dr Frederickson who was not slow in ensuring the correct papers were in order before he could convey the 'good' news to the Cordings at Grasceby.

Their plans were almost finished, but he knew there was one more task to complete before the doctor's work was well and truly done.

17: Arthur's loss

James and Sally sat on the memorial seat and time ticked by. Sally looked at the photo-fit that Harriet had e-mailed her earlier that morning. That woman could work miracles, twenty four to forty eight hours she'd said, more like ten instead. She looked again at the image and was struck how beautiful the face was.

James got up and started pacing and walking round to the other side of the church in case Lord Arthur was near James' sister's grave but there was no sign of the ghost. He walked back round the crumbling walls of the church and headed back to Sally but then noticed something a little further on, an extra, smaller grave just off from Charlotte's and Nathaniel's graves.

He walked up to it then beckoned for Sally to join him. It was clear that the church groundsman had been clearing weeds and nettles for it had now revealed the sad little grave. "Good grief, I never noticed this before, there's a smaller grave here." He stooped down and read the inscription on the small headstone.

George Hamilton Ferrymore 1857 to 1864
Aged 7 years
In loving memory of a dear Nephew
tragically struck down with fever.
Reunited with his loving parents.
God rest his soul.

They were silent for a few minutes until a voice spoke up behind them.

"I should have taken more interest in them."

Lord Arthur Silverwright came up and stood next to them, looking solemnly at the grave.

James was puzzled though.

"Hold on a moment, you originally said you wanted us to find your nephew. But here he is, buried right next to his parents!" Lord Arthur looked at them with a pained expression upon his face.

"That was what I thought when I were alive and indeed, I was present when his coffin was buried here. Before I left for Singapore, I commissioned and paid for the local stone mason to prepare and install the headstone, knowing I would not be back in England for at least fourteen months. I had no way of knowing the truth of his death and I dread finding out that it may have been different."

He indicated to the seat and they all sat down. Lord Arthur explained about his voyage and that he'd contracted malaria at sea. He recounted that in his final days, George had seemed to appear to him imploring him to find his body. He claimed he had been killed by the Cordings, who were the caretakers of Grasceby Manor after Charlotte and Nathaniel had passed away and that they had also killed his and my beloved Annie.

James again looked quizzically at his lordship. Sally jumped in first however.

"Hang on, James, you said that the Fredericksons took over the Manor from the Ferrymores. So who're the Cordings?"

Lord Arthur looked puzzled himself.

"Mr & Mrs Cording were introduced to Charlotte and Nathaniel by my good friend Dr Frederickson, an old school friend.

After their deaths he convinced me to allow the Cordings to take up residence in the manor and bring up George. In payment for doing so, George, in turn, was to make sure they were well looked after once he came of age to run the manor himself. There was a clause however that if George passed away before he could assume his role then the Cordings would be allowed to stay on and look after the estates unless I objected. Of course I died unexpectedly so I was not around to object." He studied his hat in his hands which for once he was not wearing.

"George's ghost may well have been right. But Dr Frederickson was a highly respected man and I'd known him since our childhood days. I assume therefore that something must have happened to the Cordings and he then inherited the manor as I was no longer around to contest the estate." His lordship looked deeply upset and then grew even more agitated.

"George's apparition came to me on my deathbed and said Annie had been murdered; my Annie, oh how could I have been so blind? I allowed greed to blind me to what was going on all the time. If the Cordings did kill both George and Annie then perhaps they could also have been instrumental in the deaths of my sister and brother-in-law?"

Arthur was clearly distraught now and Sally was sorely tempted to put her arm around him, then remembered it would do no good. She caught his attention and tried to look sympathetic, but going through her mind was that the person she was looking at, was dead!

"Your lordship, we may have some news for you but first, who is this Annie?" She gently asked. He looked at her then James.

"A sweet girl. Her mother, Audrey, was head housekeeper at Grasceby Manor and was much loved by my sister and her husband. She died giving birth to Annie and so they swore to look after her and bring her up well. She was educated but clearly could never be a true member of the family, so when she was old enough, she entered service at the manor. All the servants at Grasceby were well looked after and places at the manor were much sought after.

I watched Annie grow into a fine young lady and indeed I did harbour feelings for her, but I could not take her as a wife. The scandal would have wrecked my standing in London and harmed my business ventures. We occasionally exchanged polite conversation on my rare visits and the occasional personal letter did pass between us."

He smiled fondly thinking back to better times. "I always looked forward to spying her when I visited. I was saddened to discover she'd left the manor after Nathaniel had died, but George insisted in my fevered state she had been murdered."

Sally looked at James and bit her lower lip.

"Arthur, I believe I may have some bad news for you. "Sally gingerly held up the photo-fit and Arthur stepped back in shock.

"Annie... How did you do that, is it by your modern magic boxes?" Sally nodded.

"We have found her body at Grasceby Manor buried deeply in the back garden.

Some people, including James here, have seen her ghost wandering the manor but we suspect she didn't know she'd been killed.

She just seems to re-enact some of her normal routines around the manor. I'm sorry to be the one to tell you this news, your lordship."

He kept shaking his head then the church clock chimed for 2:45pm and he looked up and just nodded solemnly. James noticed this and a thought struck him.

"Is 3pm important to you for some reason? You always seem to vanish at that time."

Arthur nodded. "It would seem that the time of my death occurred at 2pm British time so I'm not sure what you mean by 3pm Mr Hansone." Sally looked thoughtfully at him then smiled.

"BST, British Summer Time, known also as Daylight Saving Time. It adds an hour to GMT so therefore your 2pm becomes our 3pm from late March until late October."

Lord Arthur shook his head in wonderment and confusion. "What a strange idea ma'am. Changing the time, most odd if you ask me. Only God should interfere with such things, whatever next? I dare not enquire. Regardless, if George was indeed right about Annie, then what did indeed become of him and is he really buried here or does he lie elsewhere?"

James stood up.

"Somehow we will find out for you sir and when we do, we will come and find you." He noted the clock on the tower was about to strike 3pm and Lord Arthur stood up and bowed to them.

"Thank you, James, Jenny was right I..." The clock struck 3pm and he faded from view leaving James and Sally alone together just as James was about to ask about his lordship's connection with James' long dead sister.

#

1865 - 1867

It was 1865 and she had cried on hearing the news that Lord Silverwright had perished at sea a few months earlier. Now she had no one to send her suspicions. Who would believe a mere servant of the manor with her claims that the rightful owners and their son had been murdered and indeed one of their most loyal servants had perished unnaturally too?

Heather remained at the manor as conditions changed for the worse. Unlike Lord and Lady Grasceby who had actually cared for their servants, the so called new lord and lady, the Cordings, were awful people who didn't care a jot about the people who worked at the manor. Well all except one, the gardener Mr Godfrey, who had been one of the original members of their household when they'd had their own country house.

Over the months since little George had died of so called fever, what were left of the original servants, were slowly dismissed, including the cook Mrs Bottomly. They'd been steadily replaced with people who seemed to be loyal to the Cordings.

On carefully questioning the latest arrival, Heather got the impression that they had been former servants to the Cordings who a few years earlier had fallen on hard times.

They had lost their estate through misguided dealings and had promised their faithful servants that somehow, they would make everything good.

Heather felt alone and isolated. Finally, she could stand it no more, gave her notice and moved to be with her sister in Scarborough. She was grateful for being taken into the employ of her sister's employer in their grand house. Before she left, she hid her notes under the attic floorboards never to see them again and turned her back on Grasceby Manor for good.

Meanwhile, a year later, Lord Cording took stock of the manor and estate accounts which were doing much better than he'd led many to believe. Something was bothering him, something he had suspected for a long time but for some reason now, it seemed to feel as if it was coming to a head. Several times he'd arrived back at the manor earlier than intended, only to find Dr Frederickson in attendance for no reason. He knew that something was going on between his wife and the doctor but had no evidence of actual wrongdoing on either accounts.

Now he was developing symptoms of a fever. He thought about what the doctor had given them to slip into Charlotte Ferrymore's picnic basket when she went off to see her aunt. Whatever it was had worked in just a few days and apparently was tasteless.

Had they done the same to him?

He wrote furiously on the paper as his mind raced ahead exploring all the possibilities with increasing apprehension.

18: Cupboards and Basements…

Joe was as happy as a lamb. As the body had proven to be over a hundred years old, the investigation had been scaled down. Once the body had been removed and the immediate area checked for any other suspicious remains then he was allowed to get back to work.

That also kept his boss Phillip along with Lord Grasceby, happy. Indeed his lordship had promised Phillip they would still get their bonus if they could get finished before Monday. It did mean working over the weekend but once Joe had explained it to his partner and pointed out the bonus would be paying for their treat then Steve had accepted it with a grin.

Joe looked across at the manor and noticed that the ghost hunter, James, was back and he hoped that there were no more surprises in store as they really needed to get the pond foundations finished.

James stepped out the kitchen door and looked around, saw Joe in his digger, waved then turned and strolled back inside. Heather startled him, she was a very quiet and he'd forgotten it was Saturday so no school for her.

"I'm quite annoyed!"

James looked behind him to see who she was talking to but she just put her hands on her hips and frowned at him.

"Not with you! Mr Shabernackles has gone again and I can't find him anywhere. If you see him will you let me know or even bring him back to me. I really am cross with him this time.

I wanted to dress him up and put him in my doll's house but now I'll have to do something different."

She huffed and walked out into the hallway leaving James to think maybe the cat was intelligent after all. He followed her through into the hallway and headed for the study where John was examining several plans.

"How are you guys getting on?", he asked as John looked up and smiled.

"Well I think I've solved why the panels upstairs on the second landing are wrong. Seems like there was a renovation around 1920 when the then Lord Grasceby decided he needed both more room for his study and more room for his library. He had two of the unused upstairs bedrooms at the back or south facing knocked into one.

The archways we see today in the library were added for effect but to also help maintain the load bearing and integrity of the walls. They couldn't take the walls completely out otherwise the upper floors could have collapsed. He moved the library upstairs which gave him more space down here in the study."

He looked at James with a wry smile.

"The original door to one of the bedrooms was where you reckon you passed into a bedroom and then shocked me coming back when I didn't expect you to come out of a wall. How about this though, the 'toy cupboard' you claim you went into, did indeed exist!

It seems that part of what we now see as the hallway was originally a small room, but again it was demolished to improve the second floor hallway and access to the west side rooms."

James was impressed. "How did you find that out then?" John looked pleased with himself.

"It was Lady Grasceby's suggestion. She remembered that there were lots of diaries filling one of the wall's bookcases and a while back she'd leafed through a couple and saw the details mentioned there. Seems they go back quite a way as well. You may want to take a look."

"That sounds good – which bookcase?"

"Back towards where you saw the toy cupboard."

James nodded and headed out of the door only to fall over Mr Shabernackles as the cat hissed at Annie's ghost walking up the stairs. James blinked and shook his head, but Annie was gone.

The cat sat down but stared up at the stairs as if waiting for her to reappear. James looked down at Mr Shabernackles.

"I agree matey, but at least I know who she is now. Anyhow, a certain young lady is looking for you, but I reckon you know that don't you?"

Mr Shabernackles looked up at James and for a moment he seriously thought he saw the cat smile. James smiled back, bent down and stroked the cat and it ran off into the kitchen just as Heather came down the stairs and ran to catch up with it. "Ooo, close call, wonder if he got away!", muttered James under his breath as he headed upstairs, entered the library and started looking along the bookshelves.

An hour or so later, he had to admit he was getting bored. There was nothing in the diaries of use, indeed they didn't stretch back to the 1860s and there was no reference to what had gone on before.

Most of them were written by the lady of the manor and detailed a mix of social gossip heard at the time of writing, the weather and occasionally that she suspected his lordship was 'playing away'.

James put the latest diary back on the shelf just as the room seemed to go cold and he knew immediately something was happening. He backed up but instead of bumping into bookcases he almost fell backwards as the room wavered then changed to show the bedroom he'd seen a few days earlier. It was dark as it were night but as he backed up he felt a door handle and turned, realising the toy cupboard was there. He quietly opened the door and slipped in, but kept it just open enough to look out.

A woman he didn't recognise was opening the window wide and he realised little George was on the bed, almost naked. It struck him that George would catch a death of cold. He shivered and realised this may have been how they had killed him. The woman turned from the window and stared straight at him and he moved back deeper into the cupboard as he heard her come towards the door. He cringed wondering what he'd say but the woman just pushed the door too, and he sighed carefully... then heard the door click. He hadn't realised there was a lock!

"Oh shit!" He muttered under his breath as he heard footsteps walk away then the bedroom door close. He tried the door carefully, but he was locked in.

All alone in the night.
In a room that shouldn't exist.
In a time he shouldn't be in.

#

Lady Amelia Grasceby came out of her room, deep in thought about organising her latest social gathering, so didn't really notice the odd extra walls dissolve into thin air leaving James standing there looking silly. Instead she walked straight into him and screamed the house down for shear fright at having someone suddenly appear out of thin air.

James also jumped out of his skin, from her scream, the fact that the toy cupboard had melted away and that suddenly he was on the second-floor hallway. Lord Grasceby rushed upstairs, quickly followed by Heather, then John and as Amelia calmed down James tried to explain what had happened. Sceptical, his lordship and Heather took her ladyship back to her room and John looked at him quizzically.

"OK, so that was weird then. You OK James?"

"Yeah, I think so. I don't know what to think anymore. Science says time travel is impossible and yet I really felt I was back there in his toy cupboard. They must have drugged him, as he was fast asleep despite the noise the woman made when opening the window."

"Did you recognise her?" John asked as they headed down the stairs.

"No, it certainly wasn't Annie and this woman was clearly trying to get George cold." he replied.

James stopped partway down to examine the various portraits that were hung up. Three were missing, he gestured at the gaps and John smiled at him.

"They're being restored and should be back any day now.

I don't know about the family timeline so have no idea if they'd show anyone you might recognise."

Meanwhile Mr Shabernackles watched them from the bottom hallway. James noticed the cat. "Oh you're back are you? Heather is with her mum but she won't be long before she comes for you again." He smiled at the cat and Mr Shabernackles strolled over, entwining round James' legs and purring. John shook his head and walked back into the study. James was about to follow, but the cat almost tripped him up.

"Oi, give over!" He started to again head for the study door but Mr Shabernackles was having none of it and again kept trying to walk round and between James' legs. "Stop it will you!" Mr Shabernackles sprinted across the hallway and stopped next to the wall then began to hiss at James. "Well I didn't do anything to you just…"

The room turned cooler and as he looked round he realised the cat wasn't hissing at him but at George as he seemed to be tiptoeing down the stairs. He had a candle in his hand and a small package under his other arm.

He kept looking about and seemed to look up suddenly as if he'd heard a noise. George almost walked straight through James who sprang back lost for words. George headed for the basement door, appeared to open it and step through and was gone.

James stood rooted to the spot mouth open then he collected his wits about him and dashed into the study to fetch John. They both rushed out, but George had not reappeared.

"You sure about this?", asked John as he wondered if James was beginning to have hallucinations.

"Yes. Yes of course I am. He was here I tell you. The cat even saw him as it was hissing like mad and I noticed he watched the ghost heading for the basement door."

John peered past James curiously. "Might explain why Shaberwhat'sits is sat looking at the door then."

James looked round. Mr Shabernackles was pacing up and down past the basement door and kept looking up at them expectantly.

James walked over and opened the door and the cat rushed through. He peered into the room, spotted a light switch and flicked it on. The steps ran down the side of the wall and into the basement. At the foot of the stairs Mr Shabernackles sat waiting for him.

With John now right behind him, James headed down the steps as the cat wandered further into the basement and began to pace back and forth near the far end wall.

There, several old barrels were stacked slightly haphazardly and as he reached the bottom step, the cat walked off and behind the first barrel.

He looked at the one just behind realising it was slightly tilted and as he reached the first barrel, he looked for Mr Shabernackles but was surprised to find he was gone! James turned back to John and shrugged his shoulders.

"He's gone! Vanished!" John looked sceptically at him but then James heard something.

Purring.

He looked around the barrels then realised the tilted barrel was tilted for a reason.

There was a hole in the floor.

Small, true, but enough for a cat to crawl through.

"Blow me down, John, there's a hole here. I think we've found where Mr Shabernackles has been hiding all this time when he does his vanishing act. You wait until I tell Heather about this." He moved the tilted barrel, pushing it back. He walked round and moved another small barrel. The floor was no longer made of stone but had two very dirty and well concealed thick wooden planks inlaid with a top covering of stone.

The hole was larger and extended under where the second barrel had been. Not only that, but he could see some movement and noted the cat's fur through the hole.

Two eyes glowed up at him and he shuddered for a moment. A soft 'Meow' and then Mr Shabernackles crawled out and rushed back part way up the steps before stopping to look back at them, startling John who cursed the cat.

James almost laughed and briefly looked back at the hole. He was about to turn away and go after the cat when something caught his eye.

Sacking.

James pulled at the slab covered plank and it gave way exposing more. He scrabbled at the rest John joining him and they pulled up the rest of the planks, exposing a set of very dusty steps. Partially covered in fine dust something the size of a young boy was wrapped in sacking.

James turned to John.

"Oh my God, I think we've found George."

19: The Cording Confession

James raced up the steps and into the hallway as he checked the signal strength on his phone. He speed dialled and hoped she'd pick up.

She did.

"Hi James, how's it going?" She didn't have chance to ask anything else.

"Sally, you need to get here. I think I've found George's body". There was a stunned silence on the other end.

"OK, I'll be there in about thirty minutes. Don't touch a thing!" He ended the call, guiltily knowing he and John had already pulled the body out of the hole and it now laid on the stone floor. He so wanted to unwrap the sacking which they'd realised seemed to be several sacks tightly bound round the form of a body. John was also itching to unwrap the body-shaped sacking and was toying with part of the sack as James rushed down the steps back into the basement.

"No John, don't. Sally, err, DS Fielding, is on her way and says to not touch a thing."

John looked disappointed but then noticed Mr Shabernackles was halfway up the stairs and looking down at them.

"OK. Does it look to you like the cat is smiling?" James looked round and spotted the cat as it turned and went up and out of the basement.

"You've noticed too, reminds me of that miserable cat on the Internet that now has it's own show – a cat of all things with its own show! What is the world coming to?"

John shook his head then they both heard a commotion upstairs. Heather had clearly found Mr Shabernackles and amongst her shrieks of delight they could just make out some very annoyed meowing going on.

James chuckled.

"Bet there will be someone scratched up there by the sounds of it!"

John nodded as James went over to the hole near the wall and examined the steps. As they'd pulled the 'body' out, rubble had fallen and exposed the rest of an apparent tunnel leading downwards. He stepped in and slowly made his way down the tight passage way. His smart phone had a torch app which he activated then he peered down into the gloom.

It was a small and quite short passage with a tiny, barely human sized, hollow at the end with three wooden shelves on one side. Several pots, a food plate and a goblet lay on the middle shelf whilst an almost depleted candle with an ornate base, to catch the dripping wax lay on the top shelf. The lowest shelf was empty but all three plus their contents were coated in a thick layer of dust.

As he turned to go up, he kicked something which chinked and he flashed his light downwards. A selection of small bones lay scattered and he realised he'd crushed the skull of whatever had died down there as he'd stepped on it. Probably a rat or something like that, he thought.

James coughed as he'd kicked up the dust and he headed back up to the basement. John laughed when he saw the state James was in, covered in cobwebs and dust.

"Don't know about seeing ghosts but you look spooky enough as it is!"

"Oh yeah, thanks!", replied James as he dusted himself down.

They both turned as more noise came from upstairs as Lord Grasceby followed by Jack Hammonds and Sally quickly came down the steps to them.

"What, wwwhat have you found now?", stammered his lordship in horror whilst Jack looked on and glared at John for being involved. Sally was about to speak when another woman appeared at the top of the steps, Harriet.

Sally took charge as Harriet came down pushing past the men and began to examine the sack covered body.

"Right, this is now in our hands and nobody is to touch the body or remove anything from here until Harriet has done an initial examination. Your lordship, this room is out of bounds until I say so, understood?" He was about to protest but looking at Sally's stern face Lord Grasceby just nodded. No one argued with Sally and got away with it, except of course her superiors back at Police HQ.

Jack looked at James then Sally with a air of frustration. "So we have to stop work AGAIN?"

"Actually, no Mr Hammond. Only here, you can continue in the rest of the manor but for now as I say, the basement is off limits."

Jack nodded, relieved that at least they could continue the work and he motioned to John to go back upstairs with him.

As they did so it was apparent that Jack was dressing down his workman but John was not having any of it as their voices faded into the distance.

James was watching what Harriet was doing and Sally came and stood next to him.

"What do you think Harriet, a boy's body in there?" She asked.

Harriet sighed.

"Could well be, but I'd rather not take it apart here to find out. Where was it Mr...?" She looked at James and he realised they'd never been introduced.

"Hansone, James Hansone." Harriet looked at Sally and had a slight smile on her face as much to say 'so this is the chap you've been telling me about', but she didn't utter a word. James answered her question whilst inwardly smiling at the knowing looks going on between the two women.

"The body was just inside what I thought was a hole but there are actually steps leading down to a tiny room.", he offered.

Harriet got up and left the body to take a look. She disappeared down the steps and was gone for a few moments as Sally stepped closer and peered in after her.

"Looks to me to be something like a priest hole", stated Sally as Harriet came back up the tiny steps, covered in dust and cobwebs. She brushed herself down shaking her head.

"Looks like it but very unusual. Priest holes are normally associated with older buildings whereas this manor is at least a hundred or more years younger than that.

Perhaps it was a quirk that the original founder decided to include?" Harriet finished tidying up and knelt down to inspect the sack and potential body. Looking up she spotted the puzzled expressions on James and Sally's faces.

"Priest holes are usually found in country houses and castles and were often hiding places for persecuted catholic priests, especially in Queen Elizabeth I's reign."

Sally looked at James.

"Didn't you find out that the original Lord De Grasceby was French and was awarded the estate but later it was given to someone else? So, if I was the one who took over I'd probably be aware that the estates could be taken away again at a moment's notice. Perhaps when the later lord had this manor built this was just in case anyone came for him?"

He shrugged. "Well in that case he was probably selfish as there's little room for anyone else except just him. Guess we'll never know on that score."

Harriet stood up and beckoned to Sally.

"Let's carry this up to the van, I'll take it back to the lab. I'll scan it first. By the way we'll have to be careful as this is about as old as the buried body and as such isn't really a crime. I shouldn't really be doing this – but I must say it is exciting!"

After taking the body up to the van Sally briefed his lordship and once Harriet was satisfied and had taken lots of pictures, she arranged for Jack and his men to cordon off the hole for the time being.

As they didn't need the basement his lordship also had it locked until Sally informed him when they didn't need to examine it further.

Sally headed towards her car but James hurried over to her.

"Any chance of being there when Harriet scans the sacking?"

She thought about this for a moment.

"I'll text you if I can get permission but we don't normally allow the public into our lab. Where are you going to be? Here?"

He nodded and she leaned forward and gave him a light kiss. "OK, hopefully see you tonight if not before…"

#

He was starting to think it was a waste of time. Every so often his lordship came into the library and asked him if he'd come up with anything or heard any news, but James just shook his head.

The fourth bookcase had yielded nothing in the diaries and indeed there were no more diaries to trawl through. Mr Shabernackles sat to one side at the window, licking himself and occasionally looking at James curiously.

"You needn't look at me like that, Mr Shabernackles. It's a wonder Heather hasn't got you in her room. You must have been an escape artist in a previous life."

He wandered over to the cat and tickled it under the chin and Mr Shabernackles broke out into loud purring.

The cat jumped off the window sill and strolled over to sit next to the wall where James had found the ghost toy cupboard.

"You knew didn't you? You knew the body was down there and you took us to it didn't you?" Mr Shabernackles looked up at him as if comprehending, then sprang up almost into James' arms, stunning him with its speed and agility. Instantly the cat bounded off and landed on the nearest bookcase, rocking it before dropping back to the floor and nonchalantly walking out of the room. James swore as he examined a couple of scratches on his arm but saw they were minor.

Then he noticed it.

A thick package had come unstuck between two heavy books on the top shelf. He reached up, pulled it out and saw that it was tied up with string. James took it over to the light of the window and sat on the chair as he pulled on the string, opened the package and began sifting through the papers enclosed.

He was deep in thought and immersed in trying to read the poor handwriting when his phone buzzed to say he had received a text from Sally.

'Soz bt cant gt u access 2 lab.' He read. 'Hwevr initl scans shw there is a bdy of a boy inside! Brkn right arm + badly fractured skull. Will tell u mre 2nite. Luv, Sally'.

He quickly texted her back but didn't say anything about the package and its contents.

He knew his lordship was bound to come back in again asking questions, so he put the package carefully in his jacket pocket and hurried out to go home as he contemplated what he'd just found and what Sally had just informed him.

Sally settled down next to James on the sofa and she looked at him straight in the eyes.

"OK. So what's this package about then?"

James blinked then handed over the contents of the package he'd brought home to study.

"It'll be interesting to see what can be done now." He replied.

She took it and carefully removed the contents and started reading…

Confession of Mr (Lord) Cording of Grasceby Manor,

November 18th 1866

I am writing this confession as I believe I may not be with this world of our Lords for very much longer. I have reason to believe I may have been poisoned but have no actual proof of this. I have taken on a fever which I have recognised as similar in nature to one that Lady Charlotte Grasceby perished from almost three years ago. I am almost certain of this for I have to confess I was in part responsible for introducing a poison to her picnic basket, the symptoms of which, I was assured would appear to the unsuspecting like consumption. Within days she had perished and I fear I have the same fate.

With the aid of my wife, Martha Cording and the assistance and indeed urging of our mutual friend, Dr Owen Frederickson, we contrived to bring about the downfall of the lord and lady of Grasceby Manor, Nathaniel and Charlotte Ferrymore, in order to scheme our way into inheriting the Grasceby Manor estate.

We, the Cordings of Wragby, having fallen on hard times, had to vacate our own country house and lands, and stay with my sister in Boston. As luck would have it, we had become firm friends of the Ferrymores and indeed the doctor. He eventually confided that he was furious with how he felt he had not been recognised for saving Charlotte and her newborn child's life several years earlier and he'd developed a secret hatred of their life and success at Grasceby Manor.

We fell in with his plan of gradually killing off Charlotte and Nathaniel and fooling Charlotte's brother, Lord Arthur Silverwright, into signing a will and testament that in the fine print would grant us the estates and manor should their only child, George, pass away before he was of age to manage the estate. Charlotte was dispatched relatively easily with no suspicion aroused as Dr Frederickson was highly regarded and it was unthinkable that he could do anything untoward.

Nathaniel was a little more tricky but his arrogance at considering himself one of the finest horsemen around helped us bring about his demise.

We were able to arrange for his horse to be spooked at Grantham and we were even more successful than we could have dreamed.

Rather than just having the horse throw him at our predetermined spot, the horse, rather obligingly, fell on him as well, crushing the life out of the poor man.

Dr Frederickson arranged for Martha and I to take up residence at Grasceby Manor on the pretence of being the step guardians for young George.

Ostensibly we were there to bring him up to maturity, whereupon he would take over the managing of the estate and ensure we would be looked after for the rest of our lives in gratitude for our services. However, we originally planned to arrange for George's untimely death after at least a couple of years to avoid suspicion.

Unfortunately our plans went astray, as the Ferrymores faithful servant by the name of Annie appeared to discover what we were attempting to achieve and she almost succeeded in posting a letter to Lord Silverwright warning him of our intentions. We were aware she had some feelings for him that were well above her status in life. Thus she was punished and I say that at the time I rather enjoyed 'discovering her' as did Dr Frederickson.

Mrs Cording whipped her and the doctor used a strange chemical that rendered her unconscious allowing us to bundle her into a sack and bury her, still alive, deep under the south garden.

Sally stopped reading as she put her hand to her mouth and looked over at James. "The cruel, evil buggars..."

James nodded. "I think I know what bit you've got to, read on." Sally picked up the letter and continued ...

...I do now, however, rather feel sick at this last thing but I am led to believe that she wouldn't have known she was dying due to the effects of the drug she had been given.

Mrs Cording suspected that George may have seen us, even though it was very late into the night and indeed he told another servant, I forget her name, of his suspicions. Fortunately she was loyal to us and informed my wife. With the doctor's help Mrs Cording began to administer small drops of the doctor's knock out fluid and whilst little George was out to the world.

She ensured he was flimsily dressed and opened the window to the night air so that he would catch his death of cold. We almost succeeded but he must have realised something was wrong as he slipped out of his room several nights later and tried to hide. We caught up with him in the basement and were puzzled as to why he had tried to go there with no escape.

We bound and gagged him to take back to his room but he managed to bite through the gag and into Mrs Cording's arm, who let him go. He dropped vertically down about two yards hitting the stone floor rather heavily with a sickening thud. Even I felt sorry for him. He was dead however and it was going to be difficult to claim he died of natural causes as per our original plan. However, Dr Federickson spotted what we discovered to be a priest hole at the far end of the basement, probably George's intended hideaway. We fetched several sacks and putting him inside one, we then tightly bound the others around his body and pushed him into the hideaway.

With the doctor's help I moved several of the large crates we had left over from a trip to Africa and pushed them over the hideaway.

The next morning Martha feigned discovering George dead from the fever and called for a servant to fetch Dr Frederickson, but we let no one else into the room. Dr Frederickson told the servants he felt George's body may be infectious so kept them away whilst we took another sack, filled it with cloth and small sandbags, making sure it was about the right size and weight to appear like the boy's body.

I never dared ask the doctor what or even who was in the coffin we buried a week later when his uncle was able to get up to us from London. I didn't want to know but I can say for certainty it was not George.

I confess this because over the last year since George's burial and hearing the news that Lord Silverwright died at sea whilst sailing to Singapore, I have begun to realise that Martha and the doctor may well be planning my own death. I can only surmise it is because I have served my purpose and I have long suspected something was going on between them. I realised a few days ago that I had

The confession stopped abruptly and Sally looked up at James.

"Bloody hellfire! I wonder if he got disturbed and hastily put this up somewhere out of the way, only never to come back to it. Where did you find it then?"

James looked a little smug.

"In the library and you know what, it was almost as if the cat was trying to show me where it was.

Mind you in the process I got scratched!" He showed her the very slight scratch marks on his arms and Sally chided him. She pulled up her skirt to show him part of her thigh with two large blood red marks on it.

"THAT'S what I call a scratch James me boy! Bloody dog had got off his chain at Short Ferry the other week and tried to hump me, didn't it? Soon sorted him and his owner out I can tell you. Assaulting a police officer and all that". She chuckled at James' slight scratches.

"OK – I think you win on that one" he said. "The cat bounced off me, knocking the bookcase nearby and this package was dislodged. When I opened it the first part grabbed my attention, so I decided to bring it home to study in peace. I guess officer, you should arrest me for stealing private property."

He winked at her. "Not a chance deary, at least not tonight anyway. You know what this means though?" She answered.

James had several ideas but she continued before he could offer any of them. "The current Lord and Lady Grasceby shouldn't be the owners and their ancestors obtained Grasceby Manor and its estate by criminal means."

20: The missing…

James came out of Lincoln Archives with a data stick and a lot on his mind. He and Sally had debated long into the night what to do about telling Lord and Lady Grasceby that technically they shouldn't be the owners of Grasceby Manor and estate. He sent a quick short text to Sally: 'I was right. Cording died of fever on Nov 19th 1866. Probably didn't have chance to finish his confession. Dr Frederickson married the widow, Martha on June 21st 1867. xx'.

He headed back to the multi story car park and collected his car. He was just about to head off when Sally replied.

'OK – meet u at manr at 11am. Gt Harry's full report. Interesting stuff eh? xx'.

#

Sally stood looking her usual important self, especially when it was part of her police work. Lord and Lady Grasceby along with James were sitting in the lounge of the manor.

"Lord and Lady Grasceby. Having discussed the cases of the two bodies discovered here at the manor and ascertaining that they were certainly murdered, there comes the matter of culpability. Due to the fact that these murders occurred in the 1860s and that there is no way you could be involved; the Crown Prosecution Service have filed the case and there will be no prosecutions.

For your information this is what we've pieced together. It is based partly on an accidental discovery by Mr Hansone of a document that appears to be an unfinished confession. It ties in with the two bodies that have been found here, a young woman in her twenties and a young boy of around 7 years old. The Lord and Lady Grasceby of the time were a Mr & Mrs Ferrymore, are you familiar with that surname by any chance?"

Both of them shook their heads in the negative.

"OK. I figured that. Now forgive me if I am wrong but your given surname Lord Grasceby is actually Frederickson?" He just looked at her and shrugged.

"Yes, so?"

"Therefore one of your ancestors was a Dr Owen Frederickson?" His Lordship seemed to think for a moment.

"Why, I think, yes indeed as I believe there is a portrait of him and the then Lady Grasceby on the stairs along with several others of our line."

"Well, this 'confession' is by a Mr Cording, a friend of the doctor. It tells how along with his wife Martha and a Dr Frederickson, they planned and indeed, succeeded in killing Mr & Mrs Ferrymore, the legitimate owners of Grasceby Manor. They arranged to 'look after' the Ferrymore's young son, George and, with the unwitting help of Lady Ferrymore's brother, Lord Silverwright, they were made custodians of the estate.

From the confession it would appear that they then began to arrange for George's demise, knowing full well there was a clause that would give them the manor and estate if he died before he was mature enough to run the estate himself. However, it seems a loyal servant called Annie discovered their plot and planned to expose them by contacting Lord Silverwright. She was murdered and buried in the main garden at the back, namely the same garden that the servant's body was recovered from the other week."

Lady Grasceby was looking pale.

"Oh, the poor girl. How utterly dreadful!" Sally nodded then continued.

"Within a few days of her being disposed of, the Cordings, along with the doctor, planned for George to succumb to something akin to pneumonia. However, the boy appears to have realised something was wrong and somehow knew of a hiding place in the basement, the priest hole that Mr Hansone here discovered the other day.

The confession tells us that the Cordings and the doctor found him down there. They intended on taking him back to his room and finishing him off there but George bit into Mrs Cording and she let go of him. He fell to his death on the basement floor. They disposed of the body in the hideaway which we know as a priest hole and there was no actual body in his coffin for the burial.

His uncle, Lord Silverwright, had no idea and allowed the Cordings to stay on at the manor presumably until he could get back from a long overseas trip. However, quite ironically, Silverwright died of malaria whilst on that business trip and so never came back to dispute ownership of the manor."

Lord Grasceby appeared somewhat annoyed.

"So where did my family come into this?" Sally looked at James as much to ask 'is this guy thick?'. James motioned to her and stood up as Sally sat down on the chair he'd just vacated. James then took up the story.

"Your Lordship, Mr Cording realised about a year later that he bore all the signs of being poisoned in the same way that Charlotte Ferrymore had been. He had suspected that his wife Martha and Dr Frederickson, your ancestor, were not just having an affair but plotting to get rid of him. He didn't get to finish the confession which was dated Nov 18th 1866.

We suspect he may have been disturbed so hid the document in a book in the library. I discovered it the other day by pure luck, and at the Lincoln Archives this morning I discovered he died the very next day of so called 'consumption', exactly the same as Charlotte Ferrymore's cause of death.

Not only that, I also discovered that it was Dr Fredericson who signed the death certificate for Mr Cording, covering his tracks. Then just over seven months later Dr Frederickson married Martha Cording and the manor has been in the Fredericksons name ever since."

Both Lord and Lady sat there stunned and trying to come to terms with what they'd heard.

Sally spoke again.

"If it is any consolation to you both, I don't believe any of this need go any further than this room as any guilty parties are long since deceased and in reality you were not to know. I have not included the confession in my final report as it is not witnessed or signed by anyone so technically it would be inadmissible as evidence. But everything fits with what we've found here.

I'm not normally one for believing in ghosts as Mr Hansone will tell you, but I do believe he and the workmen have seen both Annie and young George and the confession does appear to be genuine. But for me the case is closed."

His lordship looked at her ladyship then back up at Sally. "So, we're OK then?"

"Yes, but if you want I'm sure Mr Hansone will write up a full report for you of his own observations and experiences, as you are paying him for his services. Perhaps one day you might consider something like a memorial to Annie as she is the only one without an official grave."

His lordship nodded.

"Yes, yes indeed. You are really sure about all this? I mean, there's never been any indication over the years and the Frederickson name has been held in high regard."

Sally tilted her head slightly before answering

"Lord Grasceby, I'm sure we all have skeletons lurking somewhere in our past. In your case you can actually claim you have at least four. But we can't be held responsible for what our distant relatives got up to." She saw James seemed to have something to say and nodded as the Grascebys turned to face him.

"One thing, I did a check on the Ferrymores whilst in the archives and although I didn't have time to really go into depth I can say that there does not appear to be a direct descendant that I could find who might challenge you to the estate, so I don't think you have anything to worry about in that regard."

Lord Grasceby seemed in deep thought. "But will the ghostly sightings continue?"

James shrugged. "I have no idea. It's possible that now the truth is known and both bodies have been found they may be at peace. However, if they do continue, then, for what it's worth, you might be able to make use of it. After all, what's a stately home like this without a ghost or two eh? Might be useful to you as long as you don't let out too much information, especially about our involvement."

He could see his lordship's mind working on the possibilities and you could almost see the pound signs in his eyes. Sally looked over at James and he smiled at her as he got up and they both turned for the door.

James had a thought.

"Tell you what, I'm quite intrigued to see what that doctor and his scheming wife looked like. Care to show us the portrait?"

Lady Grasceby gave her excuses and left as she was still quite stunned by what she'd heard. She went ahead of them as his lordship took them out into the hallway and the three of them stood at the bottom of the stairs.

Mr Shabernackles sat in the middle of the hallway and watched them. All this time James had walked up and down the stairs and barely paid any attention to the various portraits lining the stairs at just over head height, but he did notice that the original missing three were now back in their rightful places. Lord Grasceby pointed at the first one of the portraits near but not quite at the top.

"There they are, done in 1874 according to the inscribed date on the back." He carefully lifted it off

Secrets of Grasceby Manor

the hook. "Owen and Martha Frederickson, Lord and Lady Grasceby with their son, Albert aged 6yrs."

James shivered as he recognised the woman, Martha, as the person in George's room opening the window at night to make him catch his death of cold. He whispered as such into Sally's ear and she nodded.

Lord Grasceby placed it back in position and they moved down a couple of steps to the next portrait. "Albert and Henrietta Frederickson with their three children, Harold, 9, Samantha, 8 and Edward, 3, 1896".

The next one was halfway down the stairs.

"Edward with his wife, Georgina and their children, Samuel, 5 and Eloise 3, 1937…"

Sally noticed something and interrupted his Lordship. "How come it's Edward and not Harold?"

"Oh, Harold was killed in the First World War, The Somme.", he continued, and James saw only two remained.

"Here's my father and mother, Samuel and Felicia, That's me there, an only child, I was six, 1965. Finally, this is Amelia and myself with Heather – that was about three years ago." He smiled as he recalled the day they had to pose for the portrait.

James looked again at the portraits. "So, they're all hand painted? Impressive." He looked again then something caught his attention. "There's space at the top for another portrait?"

Lord Grasceby nodded. "Yes, I did wonder about that myself, perhaps it was removed by my scheming ancestors?"

Just as they were discussing this, Lady Amelia returned and upon hearing them, looked thoughtful, then wafted her right hand at them and rushed back upstairs. A few moments later she returned, now holding a portrait and they all peered intently at the three people in the portrait. James smiled.

"That's him, George at the front, so that must be Charlotte and Nathaniel Ferrymore."

He turned to his lord and ladyships.

"I bet that portrait was taken down and put in storage so that it didn't remind your ancestors of the terrible deed they'd done. If you don't mind me asking, where was it kept your ladyship?"

"Oh, in the front second floor room where everything has been moved to whilst we've been having the work done inside the manor."

"Ahh, that explains why George was familiar to me, I must have seen it briefly when I was looking through the rooms the other week but didn't realise who it showed."

He looked down to the floor of the hallway then back at the Ferrymore's portrait.

Then back again.

And back. He slowly walked up and down the stairs, looking closely at each portrait in turn. He beckoned to Sally to look at them again whilst his lordship looked on, puzzled at James' behaviour.

"Do you see that there?" James asked Sally. He moved along the portraits, pointing. "And there, and there and there, in fact in all of them except the earliest?" She nodded and her mouth opened wide as her jaw dropped. James looked at Lord Grasceby then down to the hallway floor again.

"Did you know that Mr Shabernackles is in every single portrait?" His lordship scrambled up the stairs looking at each portrait again in astonishment. A cat, absolutely identical to Mr Shabernackles, was sitting looking out, always close to the children on each of the portraits. They all turned to look down at Mr Shabernackles and James could have sworn the cat was smiling at them.

He suddenly remembered something.

"Oh my god! There were the bones of a small animal down in the hideaway. I crushed the skull and didn't really look at it. It must have been Mr Shabernackles. He must have got trapped down there when they dumped George's body into it and then sealed it up. The poor thing; it's been trying to tell people all these years of what happened! That's where Mr Shabernackles has been disappearing to – back to where he died!"

Mr Shabernackles stood up, stretched, then almost as if it were leading them, he walked over to the door to the basement, sat down, looked up expectantly at them and gave out a soft meow.

The group rushed downstairs to him and as James opened the basement door, Mr Shabernackles dashed down the stairs only to wait for them next to the now uncovered priest hole. James followed the cat down the small steps switching his smart phone torch app on to illuminate the way and now he could clearly see the skeletal remains of the cat. Mr Shabernackles sat next to the remains, staring down at the bare bones and back up at James. For want of a better description, Mr Shabernackles appeared to look satisfied at the discovery.

James carefully scooped up the bones and headed up the steps to the others as the cat appeared to happily follow him brushing past his legs. The rest stood round James as he showed them the remains, then he noticed something out the corner of his eye.

Mr Shabernackles got up and walked back to the open priest hole and stopped as a ghostly version of the cat separated to sit briefly next to the real cat before fading from view. Mr Shabernackles was left sitting licking his paw without a care in the world and the group gasped in astonishment.

They returned upstairs with barely a word spoken. James and Sally were about to leave when a final thought occurred to James. He turned to look at Lord and Lady Grasceby.

"You know, it's just struck me. You brought me in because the 'ghost hunter' didn't find any sign of human ghosts, but what did he say at the time… 'apart from a ghostly cat'. So, he did actually detect a ghost. The ghost cat must have been the one permanent ghost always here on site and sometimes taking over the real-life Mr Shabernackles. The human ghosts came and went almost at random. So, the ghost hunter wasn't a fraud after all, just did his detecting at the wrong time by pure bad luck."

Lord Grasceby smiled. "Well, 'she' actually, but I won't be consulting with her anymore that is for sure. Not when you are so helpful Mr Hansone. Well as far as I'm concerned, it's been you two who have solved the mystery and her ladyship and I are both grateful for that. Now our plans can continue, hopefully without any more disturbances, what do you say Mr Hammond?" He'd spotted Jack to one side and he nodded eagerly. James and Sally smiled, leaving them to get back to work on restoring the manor to its former glory.

#

That afternoon at almost two thirty, James and Sally arrived at Grasceby church and walked round to the graves of the Ferrymores. Sally placed a rose on the smaller grave of George and stepped back as James tugged at her blouse sleeve. Lord Silverwright had appeared out of nowhere and stood next to them looking at the graves.

"I am indebted to you my dear friends. I thank you from the bottom of my heart and soul."

James looked quizzically at him.

"But we haven't said anything to you yet about what we've found out." Arthur smiled at him.

"You don't need to for I have already been told. Come, come George, don't be shy." George came from behind his parent's headstone and stood next to his uncle. "Now what do you say?" George looked at James with an odd expression.

"You're, you're the man I saw in my toy cupboard!" James was stunned.

"Wow, I thought I'd dreamed that bit. Yes, I guess I was." Arthur prodded George again.

"Thank you for finding me. It was horrible but it is all right now." James crouched down and smiled at him.

"Glad to help master George. Glad to help." George looked up at his uncle and pulled at his sleeve.

"Oh yes, thank you for reuniting us all." He stepped back and there stood Charlotte and Nathaniel, George went to stand next to his parent's. His face suddenly broke into a huge grim and he rushed past James and Sally who were still reeling from seeing the Ferrymore family.

Annie came forward from out of nowhere, picked up George and hugged him. She carried him over to Charlotte who took him from her and she stood next to Charlotte with George standing in front of and between the two ladies. Nathaniel and Arthur wore top hats and doffed them to James and Sally as Mr Shabernackles also appeared, Annie picked him up before they all faded from view.

Sally took her handkerchief out and wiped the tears from her eyes and took hold of James by the hand as they walked back up the path and round the church towards her car.

Their job was done.

Epilogue

Loch Bunachton

A couple of weeks later and Sally clearly had something on her mind as James looked at her across the table checking her messages.

"You OK love, you seem a bit down?", he asked. She put the smart tablet down and smiled back at him.

"Sorry, it's just... well, with all that business about the manor I'd forgotten it would have been Mike's birthday today..."

James nodded and smiled in understanding. He knew that although there had never been anything serious between Mike and Sally, they had been close. Especially in her early years when Mike had been her mentor and boss.

James could tell though there was something she seemed on the verge of saying but was holding back and he noticed her biting her lip. He got up and went round to her, leaning over and kissing her on the top of her head.

"I'm off up to bed, come up when you feel like it. I can see you're wrestling with something."

Sally smiled up at him appreciatively, stood up and held his hand. "That's what I love about you. You're very perceptive, no wonder I fell for you, you're much like Mike..." She stopped herself and turned to look at him "Sorry, I didn't err, mean ..." James smiled though and put his arms around her waist and gently hugged her.

"You're OK love, I do understand. He meant a great deal to you and I know you confided in him when your marriage was in trouble.

Do you want to talk now, it might help if you tell me what it is."

She nodded, put her arms around him and gently kissed him. "It's going to sound quite macabre but I'd like to see the fishing lake in Scotland where... well where he fell in and drowned."

James nodded at her.

"I can understand that. OK, let's see in the morning how our work schedules work out for taking some time away. I know I have three spare days of holiday left and Mark is usually pretty good with me." Sally smiled at him and they both headed upstairs to bed.

#

Two days later; Sally returned home after work to find James holding a letter addressed to her. She'd arranged to have all her physical mail transferred to James' home after they'd recently decided to live together and the envelope still had her former home address on it. The postmark indicated Scotland and puzzled, she opened it up.

"Oh, it's from the hamlet Mike used to go to every time he went up there to Loch Bunachton, a small place called Farrafoich." Her eyes scanned down as she read more and she smiled. "Wow, he didn't just visit them, they took him to their heart and classed him as one of their own – quite a feat considering he was a 'southerner'! Seems he solved a murder that had puzzled the local police for a year, in doing so absolving the original person accused and discovering who the real killer was.

He was made an honorary village member. It's been decided that they are going to hold a wake for him and I'm invited. I'm sure they'll let you come along too." She smiled at James and looked appreciatively at the letter again.

"What's the date then?" James indicated he'd like to read the letter. "May 28th, It's a Sunday so if we can wangle the Friday and Monday off then it would be a good weekend away. It's a long trip though, do you fancy the drive up?" James smiled at her and nodded agreement, he loved driving especially in great countryside.

His phone beeped and he fetched it out of his pocket and looked at the screen before entering the pass code to unlock it.

"Text from his lordship, they're going to arrange for George to have a proper burial and will also lay Annie to rest next to the Ferrymores' graves, alongside Lord Arthur."

"Quite right too considering they owe that family their estate, good for them?". Sally replied then cocked her head to one side. "One thing still seems out of place. Arthur is Arthur Silverwright but the Lord and Lady Grasceby were Ferrymores?"

"Oh, Charlotte was Arthur's sister and married Nathaniel Ferrymore so naturally she'd become a Ferrymore, her maiden name was Silverwright."

"Doh, of course, I remember now he did say at the start that Nathaniel was his brother-in-law, silly me!". James nodded then raised his hand.

"Another text from him, seems like he's given permission to the archaeological society to begin extensive excavations at the site of the original De Grasceby Manor so it seems it's all go since we last saw him. Anyhow, time for a drink?", he asked. Sally nodded approval so he headed into the kitchen to fetch a bottle of wine to unwind with and toast the good news about the graves.

#

It had indeed been a long drive. Luckily, they'd both managed to get the Thursday and Tuesday off as well otherwise it would have been almost nine hours non-stop, at least ten hours with some breaks. Well they had broken it into two by stopping off for the Thursday night in the Lake District near Longthwaite, close to lake Ullswater. Starting off from there at seven am they finally reached Farrafoich just before lunch after a few sightseeing stops when they were near the Cairngorms.

The B&B was delightful and the landlady, Mrs McClacken, was beside herself when Sally introduced herself and before she could say any more Mrs McClacken clasped her hand.

"Ohh now so it's bonny Sally I meet at last! Mike mentioned ya often with a wee twinkle in his eye." She looked James up and down "and who might you be then?" James looked bemused and Sally jumped in to introduce him.

"This is my partner, James Hansone. He was also a great friend of Mikes over the last year, Mike introduced us and brought us together."

Mrs McClacken took a sly look at him and then smiled broadly. "Ahh, you must be the plus one. Well if you're with Sally and you're Mike's friend that's good enough for me, sonny." James wanted to burst out laughing as he'd not been called sonny for at least thirty years but he smiled and nodded at her as she led the way to their room.

Or rooms as it turned out.

"You not be married then?" Mrs McClacken inquired as they approached the first door and James and Sally looked at each other bemused.

Sally broke the awkward silence.

"Actually no, we're both divorced but we're, err, living together."

Mrs McClacken looked them both up and down again and they both expected her to show disapproval. She shrugged and laughed.

"Well you won't be wanting these two rooms then will you. Over there across the landing is a better room for you, but mind – keep the noise down at night!" She looked at them mischievously and all three burst into laughter.

It was later that afternoon when both of them had showered noisily together and freshly dressed that they saw Mrs McClacken down in the lounge.

"Now I thought I said to keep the noise down?" She said, waving her finger side to side at them as if they were school children, then she grinned.

"And I agree with James, get that seen to, me girl." She winked at Sally who gasped and held her hand to her mouth. "I forgot to tell you that the walls are not particularly thick as you're in the modern extension we added some years back.

They don't make homes like they used to." Sally looked mortified as Mrs McClacken disappeared into the kitchen but James playfully prodded her on her shoulder.

"Told you didn't I?" She returned the slap then smiled as they sat down in the bay window to admire the view. Mrs McClacken came back into the room with a tray of tea and biscuits and set it down on the table in front of them. James thanked her and winked and she smiled back at him.

"If I may be so bold, where is Mr McClacken?" He asked trying not to sound nosy.

She gave a grim smile back at him and sat down on the chair the other side of the table to them.

"Well now it's about twenty, no twenty two years now since Billy passed away." She looked across at the view and sighed. "Seems like yesterday we buried him in yonder Kirk."

James held her hand and she smiled at him in a knowing sort of way. "I can see why Mike would take to you as a friend and why Ms Sally here sees something in you as well. Billy would always say live life to the full and I get the feeling you've had a bit of a surprising year or so haven't you?" James couldn't help but be taken aback by this but managed to keep a straight face.

"You could certainly say that Mrs McClacken, what's your first name if I can be so bold? Mrs McClacken seems so formal."

"Jennifer or Jenny if you wish as I don't mind." A chill swept down James's spine at this coincidence but yet again he managed to keep a straight face.

"OK Jenny, what time do we need to be at the old school for the wake?"

"I'll just check my diary but I reckon Ralph said it would be 7pm sharp. Now I have a few things to do beforehand so if you'll excuse me I need to get on." Jenny got up and left them as Sally took James over to the window and they gazed out at the wonderful views of the surrounding mountains.

#

It was a long night and the stories and folk dancing began to blur into one series of colliding events. Sally was whisked off her feet so many times James began to wonder if he'd ever see her again. Mind you once the locals knew who he was then several, quite lovely, ladies took their turns in dancing with him and it was Sally's turn to be jealous.

Shattered by the end of the evening as most revellers drifted away, one man came over to them and sat down clutching his glass of whisky.

"So you're the Sally then. I can see why Mike was so besotted with ya!" He was clearly a little tipsy and James was uncomfortable at how the conversation seemed to be going. "He talked a lot about ya Sally, the 'Mrs Freshman' that never was…"

A sharp voice came from behind him. "Now Angus, bite yer tongue and stop yer gabby mouth!" Jenny had spotted him heading over to the couple and dived in to intervene. Angus looked at her disapprovingly.

"Now, now Jennifer, I was jus saying he had s-soft spot for this 'ere Sally lass.

He also was telling me how he'd help fix her up with a nice bloke he'd not long met so I guess that must be you Jimmy me boy!"

James looked at him working out that Angus had to be at least ten years younger than him. 'Sonny' and 'boy' in the same day – perhaps he'd found the fountain of youth without realising it!

Jenny ushered Angus away and came back to them apologising. Sally just smiled and held James' hand.

"Mike did a good job didn't he?" Jenny smiled at them and nodded. "Jenny, in the morning can we go to where Mike, you know, drowned? I'd just like to see the place where he loved to come to, for his fishing"

"Of course you can, I'll draw you a little map as there's a nice forest trail you can take that leads to the small jetty, where the boats are hired from. Now are you coming back with me or walking back like you came?"

Sally turned to James.

"It's a clear night, mind if we walk James?" He nodded approval and fetched their coats to take their leave.

#

Next morning, with the map in hand and warmly wrapped up, James and Sally stepped out into the slightly misty air after having porridge then toast with marmalade for breakfast.

Jenny handed them a flask and fussed over them almost as if they were her children, even though she had to be in her forties and closer to Sally's age than James.

They walked hand in hand as the mist seemed to come and go. Drifting patches with chunks of blue sky above with a few flecks of cloud scattered here and there added an air of mystique to the gorgeous landscape. They entered the forest track that would lead to the jetty and through scattered trees they could see the loch ahead. Behind and to their left lay 'Creag a Chlachain' standing proud with more distant mountains just peeking over the surrounding hillsides.

The quiet solitude was impressive as they came to a bridge over a small stream and in the distance they could just see someone in a boat fishing, no doubt catching the early bites. They rounded a bend where the trees became thicker, blocking out the views but the walk was refreshing and not too hard underfoot.

Another view of the jetty, just glimpsed through a gap and they were getting nearer. The mist swirled thicker again just as they should have had another view of the loch. Meanwhile the left side of the track became quite boggy so they kept to the right and watched their step. A slight breeze picked up as they noticed the trees thinning out, the mist lifted briefly again and they spotted the fisherman out on the loch.

"I thought the chap in the village said there was no-one out here today?" Sally asked. James just shrugged.

"I think he meant tourists, perhaps it's a local doing a spot before anyone else comes in and spoils the tranquility." She nodded in agreement as they emerged out of the forest close to the jetty with several small boats moored up.

Sally started fumbling in a small hand bag she'd brought along and fished something out of it that James thought he recognised.

She showed it to him as she held back the tears.

"It's Mike's old badge, he gave it to me after he retired and asked me a couple of years ago if I'd throw it in this loch after he passed away. Little did he know he'd actually die here in it!"

James held her hand with the badge and looked into her eyes.

"You okay love?" She looked back at him nodding then she looked to the loch. Reaching back she skimmed the badge towards the water and it skipped several times across the surface but seemed to veer towards the fisherman.

Sally put her hand to her mouth.

"Oops, didn't mean to do that, hope he doesn't take offence." James just looked out across the water with a dawning comprehension.

The fisherman seemed to hook something and as he reeled it in he lifted up his rod and there on the end was the badge. The ghost of Mike Freshman turned to face them, doffed his cap to them both, put the badge on, then he and the boat faded away as the mist rolled in and engulfed him...

Sally turned to James, buried her head in his chest and sobbed for a short while as he looked for any further signs of their departed friend.

The loch remained still and empty as the mist began to lift. Mike Freshman had finally departed for good. Sally stopped crying and stood back, composing herself. She looked at James and put her hands on her hips. "Mike wouldn't want us to grieve for him and be sad. Come on."

She took James by the hand and pulled him close. "Let's explore the area before we go back home on Tuesday and remember to enjoy life. He didn't bring us together for nothing or to mope over his passing."

#

They spent the rest of the day driving over to Inverness then around and along the length of Loch Ness. No sign of a monster though, they both chuckled at the lack of it. Continuing down the A82 they had lunch at a wonderful inn on the outskirts of Fort Augustus at the south end of the loch.

They turned off the main road and headed back along the road they'd first come up a few days earlier. They passed Loch Mhor before branching off on another minor road to reach their B&B. Thankfully, Mrs McClacken had a substantial dinner ready for them as the tired out pair arrived back.

A couple of glasses of white wine later and with a new bottle of white in hand, Sally and James made their way back up to their room.

Kissing, they fumbled with each other's tops as James clumsily undid Sally's blouse and then slipped her bra off as she succeeded in getting his trousers down.

Presently they were making love whilst trying to keep the noise down so as not to disturb Mrs McClacken.

Sally relaxed, smiled and turned to get out of bed but froze with shock as she looked towards the left edge of the bed. She gasped and grabbed the bedclothes up to cover her breasts instinctively and James turned to look, puzzled at what had caused this.

His ex-wife, Helen, stood drenched and bedraggled with mud and several strands of something green attached to her hair and arms. She looked straight at James and began moving her lips.

"Find us James, please find us… but watch out for the Stag…"

She faded away as Sally fainted and James rushed off the bed to her aid as he reeled in shock at seeing his ex-wife Helen's ghost…

Secrets of Grasceby Manor

Authors Note

With the conclusion of 'A Ghostly Diversion' one would think that James's life has returned to a form of normality and indeed he has started a relationship with Sally. End of story, or so you were led to believe. However there is the enigmatic ending of 'A Ghostly Diversion' whereupon an exchange takes place between the ghosts of Jenny and a gentleman:

> Towards the back of the graveyard a well dressed, middle aged gentleman watched and nodded to himself in approval.
> "I believe you may well be right my dear. He could well be the one to help me. Thank you Jenny", as Jenny appeared next to him and smiled...

Thus intimating James was going to be roped, albeit reluctantly, into becoming a ghost hunter and helping the gentleman in some way.

And so the sequel took shape...

Unlike 'A Ghostly Diversion', 'Secrets of Grasceby Manor' is not based on something directly that happened to the author. However, I have drawn upon the experience of visiting many such places in the course of giving talks to societies (usually astronomical, but not always).

As I was reaching the final stages of writing the first book, ideas began circulating in my head about James seeing the ghost of a young boy and it seemed natural that he should be in a manor.

Having touched upon there being a modern manor in the fictional village of Grasceby in the first book, it was a short and rather quick step to place the boy there. So began the formation of the main story based on both the current investigation and showing snippets of events in the past that lead to the modern events.

I have personally not seen a ghostly boy but as a child I did have an experience with a toy room that I could never find again in a house that my mother helped to clean. That is described almost exactly how I remember it so make of it what you will.

As for the cat…

If you enjoyed 'Secrets of Grasceby Manor' and indeed the first book in the series, 'A Ghostly Diversion' why not let the world know and write a review…

And along the way, continue with James Hansones adventures with book 3: 'Return to De Grasceby Manor' and the fourth book, 'James and the Air of tragedy'.

Have fun!

Secrets of Grasceby Manor

Newsletter

If you enjoy the exploits of James Hansone as he unravels the many ghostly goings on, in and around the sleepy village of Grasceby Lincolnshire, then why not sign up to the newsletter to keep up to date with upcoming novels.

Those signing up will be the first to receive a *free* mini novel: "Lord Shabernackles of Grasceby Manor" when it is available.

So If you want to know more about the James Hansone Ghost Mysteries or other novels from Astrospace Fiction, such as how to purchase them and where, or when the next book in the series will be released, then simply sign up and you'll be the first to informed. There will also be a possible competitions or a give-away so worth subscribing to see what may be on offer soon. Note your information will not be passed on to third parties.

Just head on over to the following link where you can enter your email to be added to the newsletter list.

Note I will not share your email with anybody and it is only for keeping up to date with Astrospace Fiction books and the James Hansone Ghost Mystery novels.

https://mailchi.mp/1c69765ddf7a/jameshansonegm-signup

Best wishes and see you soon: Paul M

Secrets of Grasceby Manor

'A Ghostly Diversion'
Discover the first book of the James Hansone Ghost Mysteries.

An ongoing set of roadworks.
A dark blue Mercedes.
A diversion.
An abandoned cottage.
A young girls face at a broken window.
A fifty-year-old mystery.

James Hansone faces all the above and much more, all because of a diversion to avoid roadworks one morning. A relative newcomer to the rural county of Lincolnshire, he likes his job, his new home and loves his wife Helen.

He is also a sceptic of all things paranormal.
Until the day of the diversion…

'Wolds View' cottage holds a mystery about a young girl who disappeared fifty years earlier. A missing persons case that's stalled and long forgotten.
As strange sightings begin to occur to him, James Hansone finds himself increasingly drawn into trying to discover:
  Who she is;
   whether he can find out who or what caused her death
   and why he seems to be the only one that can see her…

ISBN 9781907781070 (Paperback edition)
ASIN: B01I83O3HQ (Kindle edition)

'Secrets of Grasceby Manor'
The second of the James Hansone Ghost Mysteries.

Renovations at Grasceby Manor
A mysterious upper class gentleman in Grasceby Churchyard
A ghostly boy
A servant called Annie
A 150-year-old conspiracy

James Hansone thought he was done with ghosts once he'd discovered the truth about his family.
He was mistaken…

Grasceby Manor stands in several acres of old landscaped gardens and had been the jewel of the village. But now it desperately needed renovation, prompting Lord Grasceby to hire a local firm to renovate the property in readiness of the opening of parts of it to the public.

But as work commences, strange sightings of a boy and a servant girl begin to occur to the workmen and James finds himself increasingly drawn into trying to discover:

The identity of the boy.

The connection to the ghostly servant.

Whether he can find out who or what caused their deaths.

And why a cat seems determined to trip him up!

ISBN 9781907781100 (pb)
ASIN: B071KS6JXR (Kindle edition)

Return to De Grasceby Manor:
and the Search for Helen'
The third of the James Hansone Ghost Mysteries.

The Ghost of his ex wife
A Mysterious Stag
The discovery of extensive remains of the original De Grasceby Manor
Sightings of aristocratic ghosts by the archaeological team
The ghost of a little girl running frantically through the grounds
A three hundred year old mystery

James rushes off to Wales to try to solve what happened to his Ex and why a stag is involved.

He returns back to Lincolnshire only to be drawn into discovering what really befell Charles De Grasceby and his family in the 18th century and a three hundred year old mystery comes to a head.

Available on Amazon UK as Kindle or POD.

Secrets of Grasceby Manor

The Fragility of Existence
A Sci-Fi/Apocalyptic tale

The extermination of our species was probably inevitable when you look back with hindsight. Every advanced civilisation has almost always wiped out the resident less advanced occupants whenever they came into contact.
So it was the same for us, Homo Sapiens.
But it wasn't supposed to have happened.
We were not to know that though.
Perhaps that is a good thing.
For the Universe...

Matt and Simone stared out at the devastation and knew it could only mean one thing... Humanity was about to become extinct.
Could they escape the fate they had seen befall others in their small village of 'Woldsfield'?
They were not going to wait around to find out...

Available on Amazon UK as Kindle or POD.

Keep an eye on the Astrospace publications section of the Astrospace web site for details of all the books.
http://www.astrospace.co.uk/nightscenes/Fiction.html

Non fiction books by the author

NightScenes: Annual guide to astronomical events for the year.

Published annually with details of the best meteor showers to view, when to see the planets at their best, conjunctions between the moon, stars and planets, special events to look out for plus much more. ISBN/cover changes annually.
A5 format, 74 pages inc covers full colour throughout with approx 100 charts, diagrams and images. Each month has a 4-page fold out spread (print edition only).
Look out for new edition every October.

Available as print or kindle print replica edition.

NightScenes: Guide to Simple Astrophotography.

This book fills a space left by many astrophotography books by concentrating on only the astrophotography anyone can achieve with just a camera, set of lenses and a tripod. No telescope or complicated tracking mount required! Topics covered include capturing: constellations, planets amongst the stars, lunar phases and eclipses, capturing the wonder that is the Northern Lights or Aurora plus lots more that can be achieved with just a basic set up of equipment.

A5 format, 56 pages inc covers in full colour with over 130 images plus tables of data and informative charts.

ISBN 978-907781-03-2 (pb)
ASIN: B07C3S9QL1 Kindle print replica edition

About the Author

Paul L Money is an astronomy broadcaster, writer, public speaker and publisher. He is also the Reviews Editor for the BBC Sky at Night magazine and for eight years until 2013 he was one of three Astronomers on the Omega Holidays Northern Lights Flights. He is married to Lorraine whose hobby/interest is genealogy/ family history and helped with suggestions involving the historical aspects of 'A Ghostly Diversion' and 'Secrets of Grasceby Manor'.

Paul writes and publishes the popular annual night sky guide to the year's best night sky events, 'Nightscenes' and the 'Nightscenes Guide to Simple Astrophotography'. Both can be obtained nationwide in the UK via all good bookshops and online retailers such as Amazon.co.uk

As an astronomer Paul has been giving talks across the UK for over thirty years and was awarded the Eric Zuker award for services to astronomy in 2002 by the Federation of Astronomical Societies. In October 2012 he was awarded the 'Sir Arthur Clarke Lifetime Achievement Award, 2012' for his 'tireless promotion of astronomy and space to the public'.

The James Hansone Ghost Mysteries series consists of: 'A Ghostly Diversion' followed by 'Secrets of Grasceby Manor then 'Return to De

Grasceby Manor and the Search for Helen'. Book 4: James and the Air of Tragedy' has recently been published whilst a fifth book in the series "James and the haunted Rectory" is in progress.

'Fragility of Existence' is the first Science Fiction novel to be published and several more are planned in the near future.

More info can be found at the Astrospace web site:
Astrospace/ Astrospace publications
http://www.astrospace.co.uk

October 2020

Printed in Great Britain
by Amazon